MOSCOW 93

MOSCOW 93

JOSÉ ALANIZ

A Flowersong Press Imprint
McAllen, Texas

Copyright © 2025 by José Alaniz

All rights reserved.
Published in the United States by Flowersong Press of Brown Ink, McAllen, Texas.

No part of this book may be reproduced in any form or by any means—electronic, mechanical, photocopying, recording, or otherwise— without written permission of the publisher or author. The exception would be in the case of brief quotations embodied in the critical articles or reviews and pages where permission is specifically granted by the publisher or author.
For permission requests, please contact the publisher.

This is a work of ficion. Names, characters, places, and incidents either ar the product of the author's imagination or are used fictitiously. Any resemblance to actual persons, living or dead, events, or locales is entirely coincidental.

ISBN: 978-1-963245-83-7

Cover and Book Design by Mark D'Antoni

To the memory of Anthony Louis

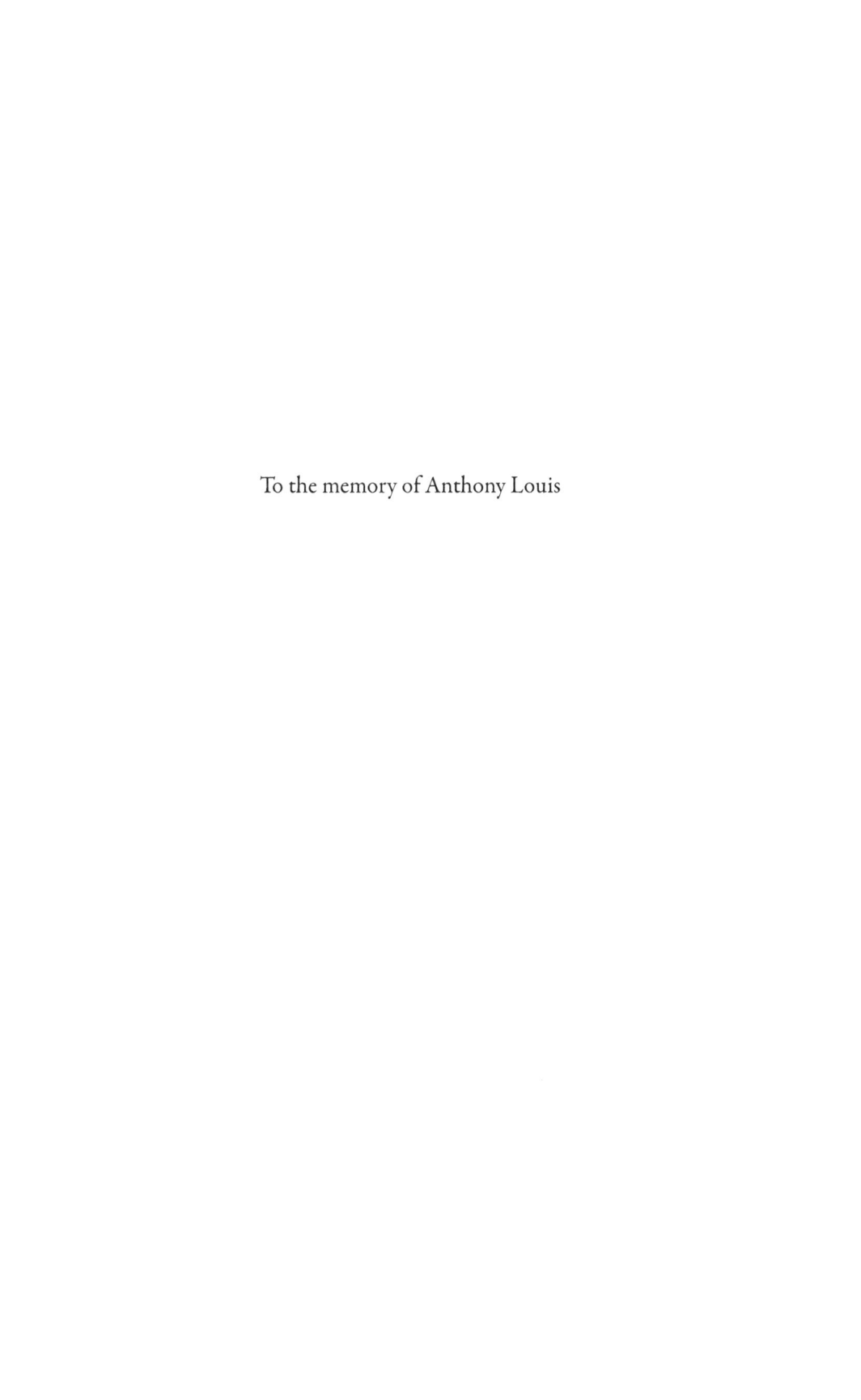

1. ОДИН

I've never seen this Kremlin...
– Venedikt Erofeyev, Moskva-Petushki

Mi cuentito
Istoriia moia

MY STORY BEGINS no-where, no-when. It emerges out of a hazy, twisted sea of bodies and dresses and checkered dinner jackets and polka-dot asses, from patches of Karl Freund lighting and Beegees strobes, from clouds of smoke with TV screens flickering through them, of *puta* perfume and the carbon scent of a bouncer's .44, an empty glass in my hand and Seven & Seven sloshing down my gullet, ice cubes jingling, and an acquaintance's upper-crust English monotone languidly informing me, "... ... I've just turned thirty."

My *cuento,* if it has a beginning, and this is a big if... but if it does, I can narrow it down here and now — why not? — to the "grand" opening of Planet Manhattan. Moscow, Sept. 19, 1993. 'Round midnight.

We were all invited, and then some.

An arbitrary enough time and place, calculated to the most plausible digit, to tell of something that never began and has not ended. But it is readers, not writers, that extort beginnings and endings — you, whoever you are, not I that feels any particular attachment to them. I pick them and I could just as easily unpick them.

Why not start instead eight months before, with my triumphant entry into Russia, in the middle of murky, snowed-in, 600 roubles-to-the-dollar January? Five years of foreign language training, of studying the *yazyk* in me and the first night in I don't recognize the title of the thin, mustached man who ambles into our dorm room to introduce himself.

Okhrana, he says, and repeats it slowly: *okh-ra-na.* It turns out, with all those hours of reading Russian lit, that I've overshot this particular word. On this night I do not yet know that every Moscow expat counts *okhrana* as one of their five or six local lingo must-haves — for *okhrana,* as anyone in these here parts will tell you, means "security."

But on January 28, 1993, in the dingy but tolerable confines of the gray granite monstrosity that will be me and mine's home for the next semester, none of us

— including me, *uvy,* me — can do aught but shrug our shoulders at this affable man (he doesn't look like a thief or a beggar — didn't he greet us downstairs?) and jet-laggedly look among our bags for a phrase book. This is because I've not yet read the papers, you see, *Moskovsky Komsomolets* or *Argumenty & Fakty,* both replete (as the years go by, increasingly so) with *okhrana* firm ads. No, instead, I've been too busy reading Sokolov's *School for Fools,* in particular the chapter called *"Storozh."* This is why, ultimately, I do not recognize *okhrana,* why my literary Russian fails us our first night in country, why I can't say "security guard." I can only say "sentry."

One possible beginning out of thousands, and not the worst. Note the marriage early on between language and locale, high and low, intellectualism and bathos, of Lufthansa-cooked college kids in their Marmot jackets and Nike hikers on the one hand, and post-communist underpaid salt of the earth in filthy olive-drab "uniform" on the other. For Russia is nothing if not her contrasts, her unpredictability — yes, that's it, that's in the final analysis what that beginning's all about.

That's why I don't use it. Clichéd, conventional — "Russia as land of contrasts, mysterious, exotic Russia" — fuck all that. That's not the beginning I use because that's not the Russia I want to show you. Though my Russia — "My Russia": the name of a moronic weekly column, a string of whiny complaints, really, in an ex-pat rag — the Russia I'm describing is not unrecognizable, not at all alien even to some of those stereotypes and things you might've read or seen or heard or passed on or ignored. My Russia, this Russia, is not, ultimately, or at least not just, the chaos/backward/balalaika model. You'll get no beginning or ending like that from me.

This Seven & Seven must be making me rambly. Or maybe it's the screwdriver I order after it from the stone-faced blond who pours, sets a napkin and delivers, all in one fluid motion. Open bar. *A sober journalist is a temporary thing...* Planet Manhattan (I'm returning to my beginning now, if I may) Planet Manhattan is billed as "the first New York club in Moscow." Never having been to New York, I can only trust the owners, Clay and Shaw, two developers from the States who supposedly own clubs in the real NY, and who look respectively like Miguel Ferrer and Mikhail Baryshnikov. The juice and vodka tastes like shit going down. I turn to Tim...

But no, before this beginning gets too solid, too unyielding, I should give you another. A beginning that is not any more of a beginning and you could say more of an ending — though these distinctions are all illusory, of course — from a time and place away from the noisy crowded club full of thousand-dollar hookers and mafia "flatheads" and flown-in models and journalists (you might say I'm part of the welcoming committee), away from the dorm that I get kicked out of in the summer, from that cruise on the Volga, from the Ossetian wine that tastes like Koolaid and the Easter service with its candle-lit procession of cripples and crones, to the day I finally leave Russia after a year and a half, on a return flight from Taiwan.

My visa gets good and screwed by a bureaucratic devotion to closing the airport transit section on time, just minutes after my flight has touched down. In this scene, this beginding or unbeginning or beginnending, I argue with the consular officer who refuses to process my request, who puts on an expensive coat and hat unattainable on a clerk's salary.

"Drug moi," he says, "My friend, we have regulations. Don't they have regulations where you come from? The states? Our hours are clearly posted, they have been thus for a long time. You should have phoned (easing into his coat).What's that? You phoned? No one answered? Three different agencies assured you we were open 24 hours? *Drug moi,* you should know better than to go by third hand information. You should plan your travels better (crisp-brimmed brown hat). *Molodoi chelovek* (plush seat slides in with finality), young man, I don't wish to hear these stories. The clock has struck and I've told you your options: stay here in the transit section until tomorrow morning or spend the night in the transit passenger's hotel, for the generous fee of only $45 USD, and we can issue you the visa then. We have regulations (takes my arm). *U nas zdes poryadok.* Order. We have order here."

Out. Slam. Never mind that in the time he takes to explain and reexplain all the reasons he can't issue me a transit visa 15 minutes before closing time, he could have issued me the visa. Never mind the other transit passengers from my flight, who had also planned on spending the night in accommodations elsewhere in Moscow, or with friends, but certainly not at Sheremetyevo, in what will turn out to be another dingy, dorm-like pension (and here we have a link to my other, "January arrival" beginning) — the same standard-issue clean if peeling linoleum floor, coarse linen, razor-thin walls, and naturally *okhrana* (a white-haired, toad-shaped woman with a bucket of soapy water) — with which 18 months of Moscow have made me all too familiar. "You should fix this," says a German fellow traveler, in English, to the Russian airport clerk at the counter. "You need to have order." The consular officer is long gone, so he cannot correct the man and tell him *u nas zdes poryadok*. The exchange, full of cross-talk and second-language confusion, between the ivory-coiffed German (a Teutonic Barry Levinson) and the clerk (a Slavic Roseanne), amuses me.

"This is not gut. You must learn to run things better now. The wall has fallen."

"Yes, yes. Before we had Gorbachev, and now look what we have…" (Hands thrown up, a universal gesture of dismay).

"Yes, Yeltsin. But he cannot do it all by himself. You must all work together to help make things better, to make them work…" His companion, about a third his age, only smiles.

Metonymy, metonymy… Nations, borders. Summits and toasts. But still, as we're loaded onto the rickety bus for our short hop to the "hotel," Moscow so near, so far, all my plans for picking up my things shot to hell 'til tomorrow, I can't shake an old sense of frustration with myself, one I've felt so many times before — of not knowing the precise cue, the subtle invitation, the codeword that the consular officer was using to solicit a bribe, so as to stamp my visa in two minutes and get me on my way. Instead, foiled by misplaced ethics and an antiquated visa system devised to incarcerate a country, I will sleep in a roach motel bed, spend a dollar a minute for phone calls to Moscow (20 miles away!) and eat the establishment's "continental breakfast buffet": hard-boiled egg, a diagonal of toast, tea in a glass and tin spoon to stir it. Russia, April 24, 1994 Russia, 5,000-roubles-to-the-dollar Russia, is this egg, this tea, and especially, this fucking, twisted, pockmarked spoon…

So, tallying up the worthwhile and the worthless of this third "beginning" — at the conclusion of which I would not see Russia again: more First World he said/Second World she said; a microcosmic (if essentialist) illustration of The Difficulty Of Getting Things Done In Russia; yer token Slavic corruption… Still all too typical, all too banal. And too whiny. Grist for "My Russia." *¡Chale!*

But if there's one thing I would like to get across to the putative reader, and here we are serious, it's definitely an appreciation of the little (and not so little) frustrations that must have figured in launching a state-of-the-art techno inferno like Planet Manhattan, a mere crossbow's range from the Kremlin, right in the heart of greedy, grease-palmed, leg-breaking Moskva.

Which is why ending number three… sorry, I mean *beginning* number three… has some merit. I insist.

Nevertheless, that night keeps coming back to me — the parts of it that will come back. Like the balloon. The hot air balloon is still there. It bumps against the side of the Rossiya Hotel, in whose bosom the neon lesion-like letters P-L-A-N-E-T-M-A-N H-A-T-T-A-N have lodged themselves: cursive carbuncles, Latin alphabet invaders in a Cyrillic cityscape, burning in the night. The symbolism is too obvious, everything is: the pinnacle of capitalistic excess, the party palace of the filthy rich, burrowed onto the hallowed, battlemented walls of this massive gray socialist realist horseshoe, which used to house provincial Soviet hacks. This very hotel, now essentially a huge cot for hitmen to crash in and screw their skanks, this decrepit den will refuse my pleas for help later in the night. In seven months the city will close it down due to its rat problem. (True.) After that they'll demolish the fucker. And here — *here* — is where the hoary-winged Planet Manhattan has landed to roost. No, this is too easy, this New York-Moscow shotgun marriage thing, this cheap trickle-down irony, it's too easy-cheesy and the spotlit balloon ("sponsored by Coors!" in English) only makes it easy-cheesier. Ah, but this too is post-Soviet Russia, she sings this too.

The synthesized bass throbs and the screwdriver splash about in my brain, making sparks fly in my vision, and this beginning — this arbitrary, unreal but insistent beginning — has dragged me back down like a rent balloon. I might as well go with it. To wit:

Between darting bodies, through cigarette haze, one can make out the decor: tiger-striped tapestries with matching modern couches and tables in the restaurant section, long Gothic candles on elaborate, gnarled stands, which contrast sharply with the disco balls in the nearby dance floor, spinning dervish strobe lights and multicolored spots. Hooker and hood, politician's son and paparazzi spotlights, all streak cometlike across the crowd. In the center, nearest the entrance, stands the bar: black, cigar-shaped, with guests clustered around it like Gogol's flies. From the walls wink several TV sets mounted at odd angles, from which twinkle *Return of the Jedi, Pretty in Pink,* some Chinese action movie, a Russian porn flick. The sound is off or masked by music; you're left to spy on these goldfish bowl universes as you would on your neighbors in the next highrise, as they feud and make up and stab an ewok, oblivious to each other, on separate floors.

We were all invited, and then some.

The models (Ellen says their cheekbones reach up to their temples); the Modies (teen proto-ravers who worship Depeche Mode); Mr. First Gay Newsletter In Russia, in his customary leather jacket and plastic snake wrapped around his neck; film festival stars and producers; bards and bimbos; middle-aged divas and pubescent sex workers; I'm trying to describe, pardon me, I'm trying to describe post-Baudrillard Babel here, get it? 20's Chicago, if it'd been stocked with uzis and metal-detector entrances and Turkish heroin by way of Azerbaijan and cell phones and stretch limos and modems and remote-controlled car bombs and plutonium traffickers and 2,147 roubles to the dollar. Imagine all this pumped into AlCaponeland, then (and here comes the most oft-used reporter's boilerplate in these parts) imagine the whole shebang "plucked up and air-dropped into the middle of the former Soviet Union." You can count on journalists for a punchy prose style; i.e., plagiarism.

And there they are, amongst all the nouveau riche… excuse me, amongst all the *novie russkie,* the pols and the molls, the suits and the wannabes, the future targets and their assassins, massing around them like pilot fish, toasting and business-carding, hugging and air-kissing: the obligatory dose of Moscow ex-pats, including but definitely not limited to the press corps.

We've all been invited to the opening of Planet Manhattan (this beginning has taken root, shhh) and I, "arts and culture" reporter for the 3rd-greatest English-language paper in Moscow, am on-scene to cover the breaking story. My esteemed colleagues and I blacken the carpet like bison, as we always do when there's publicity to be bought at the cheap rate of an open bar and an easy lay among the masses. (I call this the McInerney/Gorky beginning, shh) I mean, I know you're not the kind of guy who would be at a place like this at this time of the morning, but… you're not me in 1993, *carnal.*

In five hours I'm on the brink of death, teetering and tipping over a bridge spanning the chilly Moscow river, but right now I'm feeling warm and fuzzy and basking in 1) the club's simulambience and 2) Tim's reassuringly civilized Anglophone diction. He relates — in his calm Cambridge baritone barely rising above the throb — he describes his plans for a new publishing firm. Ever-measured, he adumbrates his ambition to build on the success of his ex-pat weekly and found a press specializing in Russian gay literature.

I will not find out for six months, with great embarrassment, that Tim stutters. It will come as quite a shock. I always thought, taking my cue from his curiously impeccable demeanor, that he was just a man who weighed his words carefully, thoughtfully — you know, that British stiff upper lip thing. Honest to God, I thought that's what those painfully long and grippingly suspenseful silences in his sentences meant. Prodigious cogitation. Consummate tact. Diplomacy, not disability. The fact that Tim doesn't let a single stammer get past those long sandy stretches between oases of discourse, I've since taken as a sign of his tremendous will —from some other age, really — to be "praw-per."

"Yes, that's… … … the idea I've been… … fermenting… over the past… year. And now that I have the… … … backers I feel I may be able… … … … to make a… mmove… … … within… … three months."

"Yeah, that sounds great. You'll have Limonov? Shatunovsky? The people you published in *The Sentry*? Oh, wait, Shatunovsky's not gay, is he? I'm thinking of, uh…"

"Shatunovsky's… … … … mmarried."

"Right. Right. (swig of Seagram's) It's cool you're expanding your operation here. But I would've thought *The Sentry* would keep you more than busy enough." (passerby polka dot ass)

"… … …"

"I mean, a weekly magazine would be quite a burdensome load for, uh, anyone's shoulders." (like most Americans, I tend to use words like "burdensome" and "meretricious" when around the English) "Oh, wow, is that Sean's fiancée. Geez." (miniskirt up to her crack, rubbery Russian legs, the softest things on earth — *morbidissimi,* as the Italians say. In two years an Italian who's fallen in love with me will save me from suicide)

"You believe she has a PhD in physics?" Ellen, leaning on the bar next to us, mostly oblivious to our conversation, outdrinking me by a ratio of two Seven & Sevens to one, informs no one in particular.

"Physics. Huh. Did you hear that, Tim? Ellen says she has a…"

"Kharitonov."

"?"

"Kharitonov. … … I'll be publishing… … … him."

"Oh, right. Gay. Booker prize. Right."

I'm fascinated by Tim, but I sincerely doubt I hold much interest for him, for anybody — a useful trait in a journalist. Self-effacement. For starters, I'm not much to stare at.

Countless sets of eyes register pretty much the same (no) thing in the brief seconds they spare in my direction tonight:

Crisp September air. The crowd (girls with overdone makeup, suave men in cashmere) pushes against the archetypal velvet rope outside the club. Bumping against the side of the building, its ropes pulled back and forth by a simian juvenile in jeans, a hot air balloon — framed now against the pine trees, now St. Basil's, now the three-quarter moon — occasionally clears its octane throat. Sponsored by Coors. Cheesy. The obligatory stage one *okhrana,* in the obligatory camouflage army uniform, gives a stolid mustached stare. (Russia has so many parallels with Mexico: armed soldiers and people dressed like them wherever you go and, believe it or not, *la cucaracha* car horns) Clutching his Kalashnikov, he glimpses through steel gray eyes an approaching pudgy pale-skinned 25-year-old in a biker jacket, of uncertain nationality, with dark hair in a pony-tail. The unshaven fat-face says he's press, shows his accreditation, and *okhrana* stage one thumbs him in.

Dark passageway, black light. *Okhrana* stage two you can always rely on for sharp suits. They see the vaguely "Asiatic" pressman, wave him over to the table, tell him to relinquish his bag. Another velvet rope holds back the seeping club noises and smells. *"Oruzhiye?"* the guard asks. "Any weapons?" The visitor, about 170 centimeters, stone-cold sober, answers *nyet.* The handheld metal detector, from Obiwan, Inc., hums around his nooks and crannies as he's asked to lift his arms, spread his legs. The other guard gives his bag a thorough inspection. There have been three assassinations by car bomb this month. The TV news is hideously, stupendously graphic with the coverage of these charred bodies and decapitated torsos drooping over the steering wheel. *(también como en México)* The guard looks over the invitation. Step in, step in. Check in your bag. The young man passes the *okhrana* gauntlet but he can hardly be said to meet the dress code. Biker jacket? Combat boots? Dark jeans? Where the fuck does he think he is? Prague? Ah, *chyort.* Hell with it. Opening night. Caucasians…

The coat check girl, all in black, takes the imitation leather bag, plunges it in its cubbyhole, hands over a ticket in exchange. The long-haired man looks sleepy, vaguely child-like. Pig-like, really. Soft. Accented Russian. Spanish, perhaps? He clearly has no money. Look at those filthy boots. Junkies…

The men's bathroom. A black urinal takes up a whole wall, over nine feet tall, quietly cascading water that gathers and drains in a trough. The man steps up to the ledge and adds to the stream. An older man, mustachioed and bald, in a suit, takes no notice. "I hear it's open bar tonight," the ponytail tells him. He pretends not to understand. Americans...

Bladder sluiced, our man, the stranger in black, makes a cursory lap about the club. Already packed; approaching 12. A DJ announces the upcoming fashion show by Petrouchka Marx. He spots Cynthia trudging through the crowd, her camera and flash in tow, pausing, sighting, aiming, obliterating. She doesn't see him, and he won't disturb her work just yet. No need. Enough "local color" absorbed for his story (his half of the story — where's his partner on this assignment?), he starts getting thirsty, for drink and company and relief from his aching introversion.

Sweet release. For there, at the bar, leaning and smoking, professional colleagues: Tim and Ellen, dressed less casually than our man, though he doesn't notice such things. He walks up with a smile and starts his engine with a rum and coke. Tim turns, notices him.

"José."

Once past the how've you beens and how long have you been heres, we all agree that the place is tacky and too expensive and will go forever undarkened by our shadows after tonight — a conversation journalists have with little variation every time they meet up at Moscow club openings. It's all part of the greeting ritual at these occasions.

"Congratulations on the promotion," I tell Ellen, who's big-nosed and freckled and looks like Hillary Clinton. From New Yawk.

"Yeah, I don't notice I'm doing anything different. I still write the same stuff in the same amounts."

(Scorsese frame-freeze: Ellen has just been moved up to contributing editor at Tim's mag *The Sentry,* whose corrupt Russian owner will shut it down in three weeks after that October business, under mafia pressure. I will vaguely extend Ellen a position at our paper, the *Moscow Post,* and use this to try and sleep with her, but she's much too good a writer and will wind up at our much classier competition. Tonight I still entertain notions of getting into her pants. Back to plot)

"Well, maybe you'll get to write more. I hope to see more of you. In the magazine. Your thing on Petlyura was great."

"Thanks. I heard you did something on Wenders. I loved that angel movie thing. But is he really such an asshole?"

"What do you mean?" (swig)

"Something about Columbo…"

"Oh, no, that was *me*. He called *me* Columbo. Maybe I didn't make that clear; they, uh, didn't edit that too well. He told me I was like Columbo, because I wouldn't end the interview. Ha, ha. He says, 'You're like Columbo. You walk out and come back in, and you say, "Just one more thing."' You know, 'cuz Peter Falk is in *Far Away, So Close*. And *Wings of Desire,* the previous film? The, um, angel movie. 'Just one more thing.' Ha. … Uh, he's kind of a creepy dude. Like a, uh, Teutonic Woody Allen. I think that's what I called him: 'a Teutonic Woody Allen.' Ha, ha. Except he's, uh, serious, not funny. Ha, ha."

She doesn't laugh with me. Maybe, uh, she didn't hear.

"But that's not the worst celebrity run-in I've had. Let me tell you the worst one, ha ha. Did you hear about the Bruce Dickinson debacle? Ha, ha. Did Tim tell you about it?"

"I'm not sure I… … … … know what you mmean, José."

"Oh, yeah. Yeah, this was back in the beginning of the summer, ha ha. One of my first assignments for the *Post,* in fact. I heard Iron Maiden was coming to play at Olympiskii. You know, the British heavy metal band. They made such a big deal about it, you know, 'Iron Maiden *v Moskve!'* Ha. I listened to them a lot in high school, you know, when I was a kid. I even saw 'em once in concert, in, uh, college. And here they were, years later, turning up in Moscow of all places. Well, you know how they make a big deal about these Western bands coming here, even if they're outdated or passé back home. Well, that's kinda what my article wound up being about. My review, I mean. Well, it was a feature/review of the concert. Heh.

"The press conference was a circus. The Russian journalists were more interested in getting their albums signed than, uh, anything else. Dickinson played the, uh, whadda you call it, the William Tell Overture on his cheeks. You know, the singer, right before he quit the band. It was his last tour with them, or so they were saying. Anyway. I wrote a review about how they were way past their prime, or 'peaked in the 80s,' or something like that, and that came out the day of their third concert.

"Their last one, they played three here. So they had time to read it before the show. And later that weekend a friend of mine tells me how she went to the concert and that Bruce Dickinson —whatta name, ha ha — that Bruce Dickinson had held up a copy of the *Post* onstage in between songs and said something like, 'Awnd this is fowr José, awt the *Powst,* who *owbviouwsly* doewsn't know whawt the fuck he's tawking abowt: Fuck you!!' and he rips the paper in half. This is what they told me. So, like, he tells me fuck you in front of a whole concert crowd. Ha. I was just home on vacation, and that story was good for some laughs."

The two of them stare into their drinks.

"... Yes, I ... suppose it... ... would be."

Ellen, the whole time I tell my story, has been fidgeting, ordering another drink, saying hi to passersby, smiling when we make eye contact.

We return, the three of us, to our drinks, leaning on the bar like grizzled vets, like an American acquaintance (such a Jamesian phrase), a 70-year-old namesake of Tim's. Unshaved and pot-bellied, in the Chicago accent he could never shake off across six continents, he told me, "José, how can you be a real reporter if you don't drink? Be like me. I've been in this business for fifty years and everyday I drink at least five glasses of scotch." He smelled it. So did his cabin, on the boat we were cruising the Volga in.

This Tim died two years later, in San Juan (Moscow's ex-pat cachet for him having soured), Acute cirrhosis of the liver. Or so I heard. In his bathroom. On the toilet, in his robe and slippers. With a bottle of Jim Bean in his hand and his ancient Remington typewriter on his lap, penning his never-ending epic about the woman who shot Lenin. On page 223. An old-school news hound of the Miss Lonelyhearts generation to the very end. What an image. Cheap, predictable. It'll never sell. You can see it coming a mile off. But he sure couldn't — could he? It petrifies me that it's what we know to be inevitable that's most difficult to avoid.

I grimace at the stupidity of that last phrase, fill my lungs with a scoop of cigarette smoke mixed with air, and heave the proverbial sigh. Bartender, a scotch. Thank you, Lloyd. My credit is still good in this establishment, isn't it, Lloyd? Your credit is fine, Mr. Alonzo. Glad to hear it. So, to absent friends. Downa hatch.

All this is a game, of course, a diversion from the insistent — inevitable, ulp — subtext to my life in this bar, in this club, on this night, with these people, as it is on so many nights, in so many places, with so many people: I am not a good "talker." I don't have the requisite "skills." I am not capable of "prolonging conversation." I do not produce "clever soundbites" or "witty zingers."

And as we can also see, I am not original (Chris Farley routine, *Saturday Night Live,* Dec. 19, 1992. He's a bit of a Belushi clone, but with all that energy and less talent, you know he'll be around a lot longer; he's not at all the burn-out type). The minutes have ticked by, too many of them, as I am informed by Han Solo setting up Leia to blast a stormtrooper and a Russian porn star putting his pants back on.

Just as it starts to get ridiculous (though the look on Tim's face, as always, radiates calm urbanity), Ellen rescues me.

"I liked your Michael Jackson thing."

"Oh, wow, you read it?"

"Sure. We get the *Post* at the office. Well, sometimes. We got it that day. You all don't deliver like the *Herald.*"

"Boy, ain't that the truth. We definitely do not deliver like the *Hurl.*"

"No, I mean your distribution is spotty sometimes."

"I know. I was trying to make a pun, huh huh."

"Yeah, I know."

"... I, uh, ahem, I liked your thing on Michael Jackson, too. It was a cool week; all three papers had good stuff on Jackson. We all trashed him. But, like, not trashed trashed. We all used him as a kind of diving board for our clever Gen-X posturing and smart-ass remarks. It was really a cool opportunity to show how alike we all think, how, uh, predictable we are. Hah, hah. I, uh, I guess that's not very funny. But you know what I mean...?

"Yeah. (swig) But Covino's 40."

"Who?"

"Jim Covino. At the *Herald.*"

"Oh, right. He wrote their rev... Right. Well. Close enough, I guess. I've, uh, I've never met him. I liked his a lot. But I think yours was the, uh, the best. I like your 'twenty drops' thing. 'Let's drink twenty drops for Michael.' We all wrote sort of 'commemorative' pieces, you know? Like he was gonna die or something, almost, you know? Isn't that weird? I guess career-wise..."

How I (almost) Survived Michael Jackson

By Jose Alonzo

MOSCOW—The following notes were pried from the frozen, drenched-through fingers of our late correspondent. They provide a fractured though eye-witness account of pop star Michael Jackson's concert, which barreled through a cold, wet Moscow on Wednesday night ...

"Michael Jackson, he's small, right?" says the Russian woman next to me to her companion. "No, wait. Prince is the small one. But Jackson's small, too."

We sit in Luzhniki Stadium with some 70,000 other people, the light-to-moderate rain slowly soaking through, the temperature steadily f-f-f-freefalling towards f-f-freezing.

The opening band, Culture Beat, finished their four-song set some 15 minutes ago - starting off with their "number one hit all over Europe," Mr. Vain- and now the huge stage on the central field is bare. Bare, that is, except for the technicians that ceaselessly wipe it down to keep it dry.

True to the latest meteorological data - announced over loudspeaker not long ago - the rain somewhat abates. But we're already late starting a show many thought would never happen, and the Gloved One seems content to leave us listening to the entire catalog of Beatles songs (which he famously bought the rights to) seemingly all evening.

I don't know which is crueler: the frank directness of Rain or the more insidious irony of Good Day Sunshine.

Then suddenly, The Long and Winding Road unexpectedly cuts off, the lights go out, and the audience roars. The vertical 50-foot Jumbotron video screens brought to you by Pepsi light up with a kitschy montage of Jackson's tour dates, full of screaming fans practically wetting their pants for Michael, to the tune of Orff's Cannina Burana. Inspiring.

Finally, in a burst of light and thundering explosions—the crowd goes wild—He erupts onto the stage, in sparkling black and gold. And ... and ...

He just stands there. Thirty seconds. A minute. And all I can think of, sh-sh-shivering, is, I'm freezing my butt off, Michael. Do something.

And then, once the cheering has tapered off enough, he starts into his set, using up his bag of gyrating tricks pretty fast- the pelvic thrnst, the manic breakdancing spurts, the pre Madonna crotch grab - while the screens magnify it from every angle.

But something's wrong with this picture, or at least, something's unusual. Despite the high tech pyrotechnics and camera wizardry, Michael is strutting among several stagehands, feverishly toweling off the stage, trying to keep it dry. They follow him around on all fours, sluglike, wherever he prances, seeming to grovel at his knees, a disturbing image of class disparity in a stadium once named for the father of Soviet communism.

But does the crowd care? Hell, no. The Russians love it, eat it all up. One lucky local woman has an out of body experience when she's allowed to come onstage and HUG Michael during She's Out of My Life. She can barely wrench herself away, but the nice beefy roadie is very helpful.

The show, considered one of the most complex extravaganzas on the planet, certainly has energy. But between every song there's a two-to-three minute gap, which Jackson lamely tries to fill - in the dark - with things like "Moscow! I love you!" At one point, he even acknowledges, "It's like ice up here!" My frost bitten feet feel better now; His Majesty noticed.

Don't get me wrong. It's not that I don't appreciate the authentic-looking undead ghouls and skeletons that ham it up through Thriller, or the rousing duet rendition of I Just Can't Stop Loving You with Seidah Garret, or even—and am I hallucinating from the cold here? - the outrageously mohawked guitarist Jennifer Batten, who joins Michael for Black and White, looking for all the world like a leather jacketed San Diego chicken furiously ripping up the chords.

I do appreciate all that, but Michael breaking down to cry during the ballads, then naming every one of his brothers (Jermaine, Donner, Blitzen ...) during the "nostalgia" section to tell them he loves them - well, let's just say I'd like a better reason to stand around in near blizzard conditions. Besides, what momentum the show does build keeps getting undercut by Jackson stopping everything, freezing in his poses, presumably to revel in applause, before resuming. This. Gives the. Show. A stop. And. Start. Quality that. Gets. Rather. Annoying.

Still, Jackson proves himself the proverbial "consummate performer" in a poweiful version of Billie Jean, and he's at his best when joined by children onstage for hymns like Heal the World. The upbeat message of peace and unity among peoples, reinforced by a huge inflatable globe and a firework finale, wins the day.

The show ends. The cold, momentarily dispelled by the show's "warm fuzzies," is back. I try to move, but my feet feel like lead. Frozen lead. My coat is soaked. The crowd scatters. I think, if I can just ... m-make it back to the m-m-metro through the ... living corridor of OMON I'll be ... just ... f .. .

"The funny thing is no one really cared about the Russian perspective. We all sort of included the Russians along with our snide remarks…"

"Yeah. Business as usual."

"But they sure seemed to enjoy the bee-jeezus out of the show. They were out there in the freezing rain, for Chrissakes. I saw a lot of little kids."

"Yeah, but a lot of those tickets were just given away, you know. People couldn't have afforded those $70 ground seats…"

"But they came, José. And all you… all we can talk about is the 'San Diego' chicken and how uncomfortable it was…"

"Uh, yeah. I guess that's more me. But, I mean, we're not writing for the Russians, are we? We're writing for ex-pats."

"I don't think it's as divided as that. We ex-pats — and I guess I'm mainly talking about Americans, 'cuz I sure don't think we're including the African or Indian population in our market research here — we kinda just come here and live this real colonialist sort of life, this mentality that we're…"

"Better. Uh, huh. That's right."

"And we think that a flimsy thing like a language is gonna shelter us. Like pissing in somebody's pool and thinking no one'll notice."

"You're being pretty militant."

"It's cuz I'm a little drunk. (Smile) Sometimes I get angry about this shit. Like this ad in the *Herald,* did you see it? It was a classified ad for, like, employment. Secretaries. This big Western firm was looking for secretaries to hire, and the ad actually said something like 'seeking attractive, vivacious, under 25. Must have thin waist.' I shit you not! I pinned that thing up on my refrigerator. Women here, to get hired, they have to be *bez kompleksov,* meaning, what, that they basically have to fuck the boss?" (Yes) "Can you imagine something like that back home?"

"Well, uh, I'm sure stuff like that goes on there too…"

"But not so openly. We're talking a major American company, based in my hometown, by the way. Jesus, I got so mad. The next time I'm home I'm gonna call up one of those executives. My parents know somebody who works at that company. Just because we're not in the States anymore, we think we can just do whatever we want, whenever we want, to whoever we want, just 'cuz we have money."

"Speak for yourself."

" … We're filthy rich compared to these people, José." (I look around the club.

A man at a couch with a carnation in his lapel is lighting his cigar with a $50 bill) "Okay, not *these* people *here*. I'm talking about .. well, you know."

"Sure, of course. I have lots of average Russian friends."

"I take taxis all the time, and I ride the metros."

"I prefer the metro. Did you see *Metropolitan?* Remember that great line that goes, 'I hope you're not one of those metro snobs.' Well, that's me. Maybe you read my two-part column on the metro? No? Well, anyway, it's great. I still think, even now, that the Moscow metro's better than any underground system in the world. Definitely better than London. Too bad they close so early, though. Sometimes I'm afraid I'll get stuck somewhere on the streets, and I'll not live long enough for the metro to open…"

"This place isn't all that dangerous. Don't get me started on this moronic 'Moscow is Chicago in the Twenties' media image thing. Isn't that totally stupid?"

"Of course. Ahem. But guess what, buddy — we're the media."

"That's what makes me the sickest. Another vodka, please. Thank you. Like this McCaffrey woman with her 'My Russia' thing. 'This week I couldn't find the right mouthwash for my dog. This place is hell.' I mean, like, what the fuck?"

I'm laughing, loudly. She's great. "How'd we get on this, anyway? I thought we were talking about Michael Jackson."

"That's what you get for talking with a lush."

Tim is conversing in his halcyon tones with another man, someone I don't recognize. His back is turned. Ellen starts on her fresh drink. I believe we have the beginning of a good talk here — and we know where a good talk might lead, if helped along… I look about the slowly-overfilling room for something to keep it going. I had no idea she's such a firebrand, such a… communist. Once hired at the *Herald* she'll write some excellent investigative pieces on the embryonic Russian gynecology industry and on the environment. Great stuff, readable, thorough. Her columns are hilarious, too. Then in a year she gets picked up by AP and they move her to China. Or so I hear. At a nearby table a 50-ish Russian woman in black (I see her singing on TV four months later) eats shrimp with her fingers, smoking a cigarette between swallows. The man she's with looks 17 years old.

"Yeah," I turn to Ellen. "I feel the same way about these ex-pats who think the rules don't apply once they cross the border. My pet peeve is smoking. Say, you think you might want to go…"

Ellen is not listening. A tall man in a cashmere sweater is waving, approaching. She brightens and kisses him as he steps up. They are all over each other. I had, as they say, no idea. She tells me and Tim that they're going in to the restaurant for dinner; she's starved. The man is older, impeccably coiffed and attired, with wire-rimmed Gucci glasses. He smiles, they go, disappear among the club zombies.

Lloyd, another one of these. Make it a double.

I turn to Tim. His friend has also left. Tim is smoking.

We are now entering stage two of the evening — a fairly typical evening, in the sense that most of these Moscow "social events" take this pattern: a) one fairly good, promising conversation, usually with an intriguing woman — of which Moscow knows no deficit; b) said conversation either allowed to falter by yours truly or, just as often, interrupted by a Tall Man in Cashmere, Impeccably Coiffed And Attired, In Wire Rimmed Gucci Glasses, who walks off with my prospective little hunka gene pool; leaving the remaining (majority) portion of the evening for c) less satisfying, often radically so, conversation, inane chatter, "spiritual" imbibement, and the likening of one's dick (as Roy once described it) to an overripe fruit about to wilt and fall off the branch. Thump.

We are young, our needs are not exorbitant, nor are they particularly novel; if you bleed us, do we not prick? or, yes, whatever... etcetera. Lloyd, this one went fast. Keep 'em coming. A wine this time, if you please. *In vino veritas,* after all, as "Blokhead" said. Drop-dead Fred. Rare-bit fiend. No discipline, no form. Does a woman really mean that much? Surely...

(... we have stumbled, inadverdantly, onto Venedikt Erofeyev territory, prose style wise. this is not at all unusual for a Russian literature bachelor of arts, given the subsequent intemperate subject matter. but onward...)

Let's move then, shall we? Tim is smoking, the bar is too cramped with elbows and vodka breath and Tim's "fag end" probes dangerously near our cheek. We can *peresaditsya* transfer — to José drunk stage two, a properly fragmented account of lost innocence, spilled cookies, and angels in the tunnels. Oh, but let's not get ahead of ourselves. This is barely a beginner's buzz. All the better to eat you, little girl.

Tim's leave is bidden and granted, the disco lights sparkle in miasmic pink — no, red, no, lavender, no, periwinkle — smoke and we have lift-off from the bar counter. You are now free to move about the meat market.

Ex-pat central. Restless natives. All the usual types: the colorful, the doomed-looking, the desperate and the desperately blessed of the great Moscow food chain. We have all been invited, and then some.

But really, now, this posturing. Drunkenness is a social construct, like they showed in that psych experiment, where ten college students were served beer in a bar for one hour and they all got merry and rosy-cheeked, only to have the experimenter tell them, that, hey, by the way, this beer is non-alcoholic. "No way!" they protested! "I can feel it. It's a major buzz!" Sorry. Nope. I would point out, with a crooked finger, that all those results prove is that college students are gullible. Not that they weren't drunk. See the difference?

Oh, all you people don't know what you're missing, not talking to me. (cue the strings) Such penetrating social analyses. Such erudition behind a gently rustling veil of disaffection appropriate to my cohort. Such Gen Mex-ican-American bombast and machismo bubbling 'neath an air of the domesticated. (Urrp) I, though, am not about to blame *los gavachos* for muzzling my Indian fire and making me a drunk hack reporter at a hack paperling, for walking in circles around this club, slowly, steadily, without the slightest betrayal of my (incipient) insobriety. I blame only — this wine glass, empty and snickering, prisming the house lights through a single, swirling, bottom-cleaning drop.

Cynthia? No. Someone resembling her. Someone vulgar. One thing *she* is definitely not, with her finely chiseled features, her boyish mien...

Ah, a familiar face. Yuri. Moscow's ace underworld reporter, and by that I don't mean the mafia — mostly I mean the mafia's handiwork. For Yuri is the city's most practiced producer of that most popular press genre: Death Porn. Murders, suicides, mafia hits — the man is a magnet for mayhem. If it's dead, he's there. (amazing how seeing someone you know instantly fires off all these synaptic connections in your brain, as you mentally, in a flash, sort, categorize, define and load up the right program, YURI in this case. the effect here is nearly sobering, especially right on the border with the sober bourne, to which no traveler returns. but anyway. Yuri.)

"*Khasé!*" he says, spotting me like a hawk. He walks up, the friendliest undertaker type you'll ever meet. *"I thought I might find you here. Celebrities and models are your turf."*

(His Russian is eloquent, streetwise, in its own way quite clever. His English is several notches below that, but that hasn't stopped him from writing scads of stuff for the *Post*, stuff I tend to rewrite for publication. It's a good professional relationship. The man is a reporter's reporter. I just sit back and wait for his dispatches)

"*Yep.* (swig) *So how is your business?*"

"*Good, my friend, very good. You might say it's hunting season now that parliament is having all these troubles. Something big is coming, Khasé, right around the corner. I can see all the pieces setting up already.*"

(among other things, Yuri is a brilliant chess player. One time he whips my ass in six minutes, and I rule that office)

"*What do you mean?*"

"*Well,*" he moves up close to me, sweat on his moustache and forehead. (Yuri's always sweating, even in winter.) "*You know about the 'snow drops.'*"

"*Um, yes. I believe this is the dead people in the snow?*"

"*Right. The corpses found in Spring after the snow melts. Often they lie there for six months, frozen. Well, this year the snow drop season is starting early. These political problems are going to contribute to the harvest, in a big way.*"

His eyes are lit up. It must be the disco lights. The liquor is fucking with my sensations. I get a shudder up my back.

"*Are you, uh, going to write something for us?*"

He steps back. The eyes darken.

"*Perhaps. That porcine* (?) *publisher of yours is a difficult man to deal with.*" He responds coolly, pushing the upper threshold of my Russian vocabulary. "*But there are always arrangements that can be made. I was quite miffed* (?) *about that bus fire debacle* (?), *but now… we shall see, my friend.*"

He's staring around the club, as if keeping some prey in sight. The man lives for the chase. Or more exactly, for the carcass.

The bus fire.

I'm at the office, working on a deathly dull government banking policy story (this is about three months ago).

Kyleigh, our 40-something Iowan managing editor, steps into the office to the rescue.

"José, buddy boy, drop what you're doing. We got Yuri on the phone for ya. We'll run that page 6 filler tomorrow. Line 2."

"Yes ma'am."

I close the article, two paragraphs that have taken an hour each to write, thanks to busy phone lines, uncooperative interviewees, a scrawny press release, and sheer boredom. With a flourish I reach for the line 2 button, flashing Batphone red, press it and recline, ready to sink my teeth into real meat. Literally. *Al carbone.*

"*Yuri! Privet!* (a horribly crackling line — some public phone. There's traffic and confused noises behind his voice.) *What's that?... Right... Dmitrevskoye... near the railway station* (scribble, scribble)*... uh, huh... Oh, wow... How many?... At least six? My God. How'd it happen?... ... Incredible. Were there any witnesses? To the truck passing, I mean?... What does* 'obnazhyonniy' *mean?... Oh, right. Gee... ... Hey, you're safe, right? You're not too close?... That's why I'm asking. With another reporter I wouldn't worry... ... Ha, ha. I bet... ... You think so? The TV news?... Uh, huh... well, I'm sure* the Hurl *will... Ha, ha! Right... You'll bring pictures?... Yeah, yeah, I'm sure... Sure... What do the cops say?... Uh, huh. Uh, huh. Figures..."*

We go on like this a few more minutes, piecing together our little Frankenstein article with a who here, a what there, some hows and why's and whens and what fors. Add a little wire service detail for padding, and BOOM! Your standard 600 words on your standard run of the mill urban tragedy.

Around quarter to six Yuri bursts into the office, like he always does, bringing in some sensationalist piece that Anthony usually runs. The man is ye certified master of the macabre. His shirt is soaked with sweat.

"*Khasé! There you are!*" he says in Russian. He comes up to my desk, clutching a manilla envelope. "*They're right here. Fresh and ready.*" He makes a reference to a poem, I think, or a Soviet movie, something I don't pick up.

"*What?*" (he catches me in the middle of another article, in the typists' room 'cuz all the other computers are taken.)

"*The photos, my friend, the photos. I did more than kiss widows and orphans* (?). *Everything went well, right?*"

Kyleigh, seeing Yuri, approaches us.

"Whadda you got there, Yoori?" she asks. Then she sees. "Oh my lord!"

"You like, no?" He's switched to English for Colleen, and he's pulled out a batch of seven or eight glossies, still smelling of developer.

Carnage. The words I've been typing, the descriptions I've tapped up neat and clean all afternoon, suddenly shrivel up and die, crushed, atomized by these obscene photos. The bus. The black dangling limbs. Etcetera. Death Porn.

The worst is the picture of a woman, burned alive, lying like a toppled statue on the street. That's the texture the black and white photo gives her: a grainy, cementlike coating over a fat, middle-aged *baba,* the thick-calved kind you see everywhere you turn in Moscow, her top layers of flesh charred off in agony. He has three pictures of her, and in all of them the most chilling detail, the part that, for some unfathomable reason, most twists my stomach, is the umbrella. The woman died in flames, some ten meters from the bus, still holding her umbrella.

"She, how to say, fisted out a window," Yuri says, a mischievous gleam in his eye, sweat drops on his lip. "Heh, heh. Battered out, fought off other, mm, passengers. Yes. She fell out of the space, and runned and runned down the street, with fire eating her, eating her. She yelled a lot. And then, all of an instant, she falls to the down. Nobody comes close to her until she stops to move. Heh, heh. Is good angle here, right? People in background. The police man told me she had three kids, and a drinking man husband. Her kids say later on TV that she was to bringing to home the beer that he was to making her to buy. You are sure we cannot to use these shots, Khasé? I was very lucky to be nearby when it occurred. They, ah, are shots most excellent, no? *Exclusivny!*"

"They're great, Yuri. I'm gonna to go to throw up now."

"*Chevo?*"

"Yoori," Kyleigh says, in a monotone. "There's no way we're runnin' these pictures." The whole typing room has come to a standstill. The typists and editors are poring over the photos, grossing out, pretending they don't want to see but seeing with wide eyes.

"No to run? What, mm, to say Anthony?"

"Well," she says, "You can go ask him, but if he runs these pictures… I don't know. I'm quitting. I'm defacto photo editor and this… this… trash is unacceptable."

"Trash? What is this trash? You not like?"

Kyleigh has turned away, snatched the photos from Natasha's hands, stuffed them in Yuri's envelope. "Thanks for your reporting. You did good." And she sits back down at her computer.

Poor Yuri's a little lost.

"You wanted photos, no? I tooked them. I was, mmm, how to say, mmm, fortunate to be close when this occurred. I got good photos, no? Anthony will like?"

Kyleigh's not looking at him. The typists are back at their places. I'm just sitting there.

"They're good photos, Yoori, but not for this newspaper." She starts typing.

THE MOSCOW POST

Ten Dead in Fiery Crash

By Jose Alonoz and Yuri Presidentov

MOSCOW—At least 10 people died and 24 were injured on Thursday in a grisly fire caused when a cargo truck collided with a fuel tanker lorry, spilling gasoline onto a busy intersection at midday and trapping a trolley-bus full of travelers in flames.

The catastrophe occurred at Dmitrevskoe Highway and Ulitsa Vagonoremontnaya, not far from Savelovsky Railway Station. The driver of the cargo truck, who was stopped at a red light, tried to manoeuver his vehicle around busy midday traffic, punching a hole in the fuel carrier's tank, said witnesses.

Petrol leaked under the trolley-buses — two empty, one full of people — and empted in flame.

Three trolley-buses, one bus, and several other vehicles were completely burned down within eight minutes, according to Russia's State Committee for Emergency Situations. Victims were evacuated to several local hospitals and 13 fire trncks arrived on the scene within 30 minutes.

The exact cause of the fire was unknown, although at least one policeman said electric sparks from the trolley-bus' cables started the blaze, reported Reuters.

"The hatch of the tanker burst off and fuel spurted on to overhead cables of three trolley buses," said SCES chairman Yuri Sharykin, according to Reuter. "Fire spread from one to another."

The driver of the cargo truck, Vitaly Frolov, a worker with Odintsovsky Transport Enterprise, was arrested, said GAI department head Sergei Moiseyenko.

Policed sealed off the area while firefighters felled burning trees and contained the conflagration. Police held back journalists and told photographers their film would be destroyed if they tried to violate the cordon.

Nonetheless, Russian television broadcast horrific images of burned corpses and wreckage, and initially claimed that "dozens" had died.

Witnesses described a scene of panic as the crowd within the trolley-bus struggled to escape the flames. One woman managed to jump out of a window, but she was already on fire and died on the asphalt.

Victims were rushed to Sklifosovsky, Botkinskaya, and other hospitals.

Authorities placed the time of the accident at 11:46 a.m. Firefighters had extinguished the blaze by 12:15pm.

Yuri stands there, holding his envelope, with a look on his face like he's solving a stubborn equation (he was a physicist at a military research center in the waaaay back then two years ago, before he turned to journalism). Then he brightens. He's solved it.

"Color? You to want there to be color? Color you want?" he says, grinning. "I had with me a color camera as well! I will to make them at Moskva! *Khasé, obyasni yei! Explain to her that I'm going to develop my color photos at the Moskva Department Store.* (It's a short walk away.) *What's the deadline, 7 p.m.? I'll be back in half an hour! No problem!*"

And he rushes out. In the end, Anthony doesn't run his photos, color or black and white, and we hear through the walls the usual shouting match over payment, lost time, lost exclusive rights, etc.

Me, I stay pretty numbed out the rest of the day.

"You're lookin' a little white there, José," says Danny, from behind his printouts. Sports editor. Refugee from Cleveland. "You want me to put on some Ween to cheer you up?"

I tell him I'm alright. I gather my things for home. Another fine day's work. A postscript. Yuri makes a killing on his pics anyway, selling them to various Russian tabloids for which he also writes. His photos run off and on for over a week. I hear the publishers give him a bonus for almost doubling sales during that period. But he won't write for the *Post* again for several months.

"Perhaps later we can chat more," Yuri says, taking a vodka on ice from a passing tray. It sweats, like him, as he puts it to his lips. *"Right now I have my quarry (?) to hunt down."* His gaze is fixated on something at the other end of the club.

"Are you, um, working?"

"Professiya takaya, my friend. Such is our line. Tonight I am — how do you Americans say it? 'Expecting rain.' *You see that bald Jew sukinsyn, that sonofabitch with the blonde? My sources tell me he won't live past four a.m. I've been guaranteed an on-the-spot exclusive as long as I don't lose sight of him."*

"Are you... uh, are you in seriousness talking?" (the liquor makes me the teeny-tiniest bit wobbly at the knees) *But... could you not, uh, warn him? This man's life is in your hands, no?"*

Yuri turns his eyes to me, without turning his neck. He inspects me, a Hannibal Lecterish once-over that makes me just an eensy-weensy bit unsteady.

He laughs, hale and hearty, puts his arm on my shoulder.

"*You're drunk, my friend. And melodramatic. That's what makes you valuable to your field.* (he finishes the vodka, in one gulp) *My field requires other skills. I must go. By the way, I enjoyed your Michael Jackson piece. Reading you, I think, is helping my English. A word of advice* (he grips my hand, shakes it, the friendliest gesture you could imagine): *don't mix the libations* (?). *Stick to vodka. I don't want you to turn up at Gorky Park next Spring when the snow melts, all thawed-out and half-rotted. But if you do,*" he's walking away, a beatific grin, "*will you let me have first rights to the story?*"

I give him the hand-shaped-like-a-gun "You got it!" sign, cluck my lips.

The room is starting to blur and spin — not unpleasantly. But I'm thirsty. I need a drink. Yuri has disappeared into the crowd, which seems to be thickening even more, arms and cell phones and silicone hanging out everywhere.

Soon the Fashion Show comes on, and we all gather by the raised disco floor to watch gaunt Russian models with idiosyncratic cellulite prance about in pastels and Escher rip-offs, to the beat of that "A-a-a-ll That She Wants Is Another Baby" thing, in like thirty different dance versions. Next to me, an old man in a tuxedo *(russus post-sovieticus luzhkovus)*, who can barely stand (he reeks of vodka and — is that urine?), whips out a huge bundle of hundred-dollar-bills, the size of a cantaloupe.

"*You!*" he shouts at a model in a swimsuit. "*I'll give you a shtuka to take it off! You there! Yes! A shtuka for your tits!*"

A *shtuka*, what Peorians would call one thousand simoleons, flitters in the man's spasmodic hand, at the end of his waving arm. The model, a buxom beauty practically falling out of her two-piece, turns to look down at him. The crowd backs up the geezer. Others start bidding up the price of her mammaries.

"*Two shtuki!*"

"*I'll give you poltara for each!*"

"*Come on, slut! Show them to us.*"

The fashion routine is a little compromised. The other girls behind her stop their catwalking while she stands there, in her swimsuit, shades and wide-brimmed hat, looking at the crowd. The music barrels on. Her face has no emotion.

"*This is isn't Lis's, you know,*" she says, in a gravelly voice. "*Why don't you go there if that's what you want?*"

The other models start to argue with her, telling her to go ahead so they can get back to the show. They all have work to do. The crowd works itself up to a higher pitch. I see Clay, the co-owner, standing nearby, smiling, nodding timidly to his companions — but his eyes are those of a trapped hamster.

Finally, the woman pulls off her top, and the crowd goes wild. They are indeed the finest set of breasts I've seen in quite a while: aureolas the size of kopecks, the color of Georgian wine. She looks to be from the Caucusus. Flashing her yellowed, irregular teeth, the girl is showered with money, like confetti, like ejaculate. She gathers the bills to the distinct ire of her colleagues on the stage — their assets are *"po-menshe."* Littler. Turns out our Georgian princess was being coy just to raise the bids. Ah, the free market.

The 'avant garde' portion of the fashion show treats us to effete men and women dressed up as Dalmation-like polka-dotted scissors, with matching facial make-up. One flustered-looking man is apparently representing paper: he drags along a huge sail-like sheet, propped up with sticks, in which he is embedded, as the others try to "cut" him. I am not making this up. Such is the phrase that somehow finds its way inside my somewhat-addled brain, from some memory of a sportscaster in the States. So far and yet so here, in spirit.

The *spektakl* closes with a rousing rendition of *Puttin' on the Ritz* — the Taco version — played at booming concert volume and lip-synched by a trio of unknowns in dinosaur costumes. Barney-like, they dance and pirouette through the crowd, tossing Planet Manhattan coozies and matches. This is a treat; usually monsters are only trucked in for restaurant floor shows. Clay and Shaw have outdone themselves. Someone has let a dog in, a big doberman on some goon's leash, and it barks and growls at the saurians. An eerie, a Lynchian sight: such a large dog barking at full blast, and not being able to hear it for the music. Especially when it's barking at a saggy-titted tyranno with a microphone. But let's not poison the well. We can all judge for ourselves. The final notes ring out, tingling on in our ears, and the dinos unceremoniously lumber off. One of them is already taking off its head — a gaunt girl, dripping.

We need to wet our whistles after that. Another round, another round. Last one. Seven & Seven again, please, my good man. Thanker, *spasibo*. To the... to the snow drops. Cheers. Whoa! Gettin' a little wobbly-tobbly there. And so we arrive at

Stage three. There seems to be a steep downward curve with this liquor. Slippery slope. More fragments, more disassociation, broadly speaking. The Russians have a saying, *"My vstretimsya pod stolom."* "Under the table we'll meet." I shall now demonstrate.

Vova, how the hell are you.

"Khasé! Good to see you here. You got the passes, then. This is Anya. Did you enjoy the fashion show? Superb, no? And the Ace of Base was quite an original touch, very *klassno*. Like London, the Hippodrome, I should say, eh? And this club, amazing — it's like I'm in New York, at least what New York should be, right?"

(Some context. Vova, before moi's arrival, was the "arts and culture" reporter — or more accurately stringer, he wasn't on staff — for the *Post*. On my first major "arts" assignment, an Iron Maiden concert — yes, *that* Iron Maiden concert — we clashed at the press conference. He didn't know who I was, only that I was barging in on his turf. Not too auspicious. Since then we've each carved our niche at the paper and don't really cover each other's field, so things are hunkey-dorski. We're quite chummy, in fact, and he often comes through with passes, invites, accreditations. He likes writing about "modern dance feminist rave techno" — at least that's what he calls it — and stereo components. He fancies himself a sort of "rock journalist" — though his writing invariably engenders laughter and the heebie-jeebies among our all-female editors. Suki, for example, says she's framed a couple of his raw submissions, pre-rewrite, on her apartment wall, as phantasmagoric masterpieces of horribly mangled English, hilarious metaphor and pedophilic fantasy. But here we go again, poisoning the well.

A physical description? But with of course. Shape like of a pear being, about late thirties, teeth of the Soviet-era dentistry variety surviving, of the head with oily love potion balding. But the nicest of the chaps to meet you would have liked in history, if harried-looking slightly. Friend good that it would being cheap and insensating would be to like this unflatulatingly to describe if sober were being. All knowing this, I like wild hot hog to the above conversation retread in blaring sunlight of new backgrounding info and the blanks to be filled)

Vova, how the hell are you.

"Khasé! Good to see you here. You got the passes, then. This is Anya. Did you enjoy the fashion show? Superb, no? And the Ace of Base was quite an original touch, very *klassno*. Like London, the Hippodrome, I should say, eh? And this club, amazing — it's like I'm in New York, at least what New York should be, right?"

Metal to the Madonna Moon by Vladlen Bovryov
Special to the Moscow Post

New Russian videos are to be daily arriving in stores every day.

My favorite right now to be seen of them is of the new variety Zhanna Alisa, the pop-temptress many being in the Russian Federation say will be the next Madonna Ciccione, the "blonde bombsheller." Unlike the tacky as a Russian bear being abusive to himself in the great open nature Kostia Kinchev, who only takes only himself seriously, this Alisa owns Roman legions of hot and heavy girls (of 12, 13 age groups) who go wild like heated enchantress hogs at her concerts selling out.

Many of these delicious Nabokovite "nymphets" appear in the video "Rock Around the Kremlin" giving the ecstatic-driven moon looney viewer the deep and moist impression that the jolly fairies will lead you down a thoroughfare where a oily love potion is been for you prepared.

I listen to Alisa on my Sony CRX-2218 system of hot components, polished smoothly as if strokened in a repetition with the oily love potion afforementioned. I in plunge the video of new Alisa clips deep into my manly black Aiwa XL-30 model vcr, to watch long hours of her fans going me crazy with excitement music in their attired that barely their hips and thighs and bosoms oily like my Sony covered. Do not keep your loins still for this but dance it is impossible to stop and stop.

For much ecstasy, buy this recommmended highly video, especially the clip "My Little Runaway," being familiar to the fans of Benny Hill and his "Angels." In the clip, Alisa is being attired as Darryl Hannah attack of the Fifty Feet Woman, a controversial footage.

A lot of smoke and whorror. For a croon and spoon, Vova gives to it whole five stars entire. Only one slight reservoir. Next time, Zhanna, bring more wild as hogs fangirls, screaming scratchily in crowds! Thanks to the God for control of the "PAUSE" image.

"That was a wonderful piece on that woman singer, Vova, really."

"You think so? I'm never sure of my English, but I study my Rolling Stones all the time and I read your column. I try to keep my language lively like superb flashy American style, but I'm never sure…"

"No problem, my friend. It's (hic) great work. *We all like it in the office and we are being very grateful you're to be writing it."*

"I'm very happy to hear that, Khasé. Sometimes, you know, it's difficult. Slozhno.

Complicated. Your Russian is superb as well. (he likes "superb." triple underline) Isn't it Anya? Have you ever heard a foreigner like this? Superb."

"I don't know." The woman, far from being a nymphet, looks older than Vova. Peroxide blonde, tiger-striped leather hot pants. She matches the wall hangings.

"Vova, I have thirst. Later I will to see you and Alisa?"

"Anya. Yes, of course. I'm glad you could come."

"I would not have being missed it for the planet. Ciao."

Back at the bar. I don't know what I'm drinking. It's tart. My mouth is getting numb. Ellen, you bitch. Tim is talking to me. Things in full swing, like the center of a carousel. Notime, nowhere. *Okh-ra-na. Let me get my phrase book.* No. Tim. Tim is talking. Concentrate. Quilty, concentrate. You're going to die. He's answering a question I posed, somewhen, somehow, about whose content I have no idea. How meretricious of me. His answer starts — or does it conclude? — with

"… … I've just turned thirty."

At any rate, this is the phrase, the expression, the loop, that keeps playing and after-imaging on and on like a house of mirrors or (more proletarian if you like) a barber shop's mirrors.

Somehow my head feels too large to fit in my head. I wander. Life is a journey, sha-boom. A porn star is coming into a bowl of borscht. *Do the Right Thing* has light-sabered *Star Wars* off the screen. A couple of American guys are talking to me. One's leaning against the wall, in a polka-dot white leather jacket. He writes for *Village Voice,* he says, I think. He seems scared of me. A flimsy little poddle-haired guy, wearing his jacket like a turtle shell, swallowed in it. I do believe he's afraid of me. Every time I take a half-step towards him, he pulls back, cringes against the wall.

"Yeah, I'm here for the opening. We flew in this morning. Oops! Careful. ... gay bars. I said GAY BARS! I'M RESEARCHING RUSSIAN GAY BARS! What's that? The Underground? By who? Kalinin? How do you spell that? Oh, yeah, the guy with the snake wrapped around his neck. Yeah. I saw him. Oops! Watch it. I said OOPS! WATCH IT! Where? Yeah that would be great. But where did you say...? Across from what? The Pushpin Museum? They have a pushpin museum here? How do you spell that? P-U, uh huh, S-H-K-I-N. Okay. Oh, right. From the sixties, right? ... shenko, right? LIKE YEVTUSHENKO, RIGHT? THANKS. I'll check it out. Oh, only 'til Sunday. I was a college friend of Clay's. You think he looks like who? Oh, right. Yeah. RIGHT! Well, I don't know. But they say they're in it for real. Moscow's pretty trendy right now. The fall of the wall and everything. It's like the whole country's been outed. I SAID OUTED! Right. Uh, listen, I better go. GO!. Nice meeting y..."

The other guy? He's gone. All I remember is he writes for some show.

Yeah. Spinning. A little tired. Somewhere far away. SOMEWHERE FAR AWAY! I better go now. See you la...

At last. Thank you, God. Cynthia. Much better.

"How long have been sitting here?" She sits opposite, the candle-light stoking her feline eyes like the scoreboard bobcat at my high school football stadium. Whenever our team scored, the eyes on this giant bobcat head would... oh never mind.

"Mm not sure. What happened to the woman who was sitting here?"

"I think she's the one that got away, ace."

"I'm more interested in my current company."

"You're a little buzzed, aren't you? Who'd you come with?"

"... uh... um... Me, myself and *ya*."

"You can relax, José. You don't have to think of a clever remark every time I ask you a question. I'm not sleeping with you anyway."

"Then what're you here for?"

She looks at me like I just threw a shit pie at 'er. Retreat. Retreat.

"I'm sorry, Cynthia. I don't know why I said that. Yeah, I'm a little... a little..."

"Right. Look, maybe you better get home. Vasily and I are all done here, too."

"Oh, Vasily. Right. You gonna get much for this job?"

"Well, we have to split it as usual. But it's something to tide me over 'til I get to the Caucusus, Dagestan or something."

Cynthia and I met through one of those thoroughly uninteresting people who seem to be a nexus by which other more interesting people meet each other. Cynthia takes pictures. She wants to cover "hot spots." In this respect she is like lots of ex-pat journalist thrill-seekers in Moscow. But that's not why I like her. That's not why my sore and bruised heart says,

"So you and Vasily are gettin' pretty friendly, huh?"

Her eyes to me. Meow.

"Please. Not my type. You know who I like? I was just in the states, and I gotta go back next week. But anyway, I was just there and... have you seen *Much Ado About Nothing?* Denzel. Denzel Washington. I think he's so hot."

"Yeah, I saw it. It opened at the Ameruss House of Cinema couple'a weeks ago. Yeah, Denzel's, uh, hot."

Escalator. Metro station escalator. Did she tell me this on an escalator? Did the Planet Manhattan conversation take place at all? Did she conclude it by saying she'd come back for me so we could go to the metro together? Did she opine that I might need someone to take me "in" in "my" "condition"? Did she not mention Denzel Washington after a play, before leaving her off after a quick taxi ride, without her inviting me in? Is that what happened? Was she ever in that empty chair, glowing brighter and darker in the candle light? Will any of this be? Which version, which lie? Like this? Will it happen like this, four months hence? Will I ask her out again? Will it be anything like this? Look, listen, like this:

The last time I see her I stay over at her place, in between residences. She's got business again back in New Yawk, this is the night before she leaves. But she'll be back, back to stay. She's not going to miss another October 3, goddammit. She's still angry about that: out of town on the biggest news weekend of the year, hell, the decade, when tons of freelance photographers make their names during this once in a lifetime opportunity. Not again. I'm better than them, José. I'll do what it takes to get a better shot. I'm better than shooting ribbon cuttings and club openings and shit. I'm better than that. I want the hot spots. That's what I want. I'll do what it takes.

Her living room. Romantic lighting. Wine. She shows me her gory left toe. "I gouge them," she says.

"Gouge them?"

"Yeah. I can't help it. I'll be cutting them with a clipper and I get down to the cuticle, but I just can't stop. I keep going, 'till I'm cutting skin, bleeding."

"But why do you... do that?"

She smiles, bright green cat eyes.

"I don't know. I just do it. Sometimes I gouge 'em so bad that I can't walk. This isn't so bad tonight."

"I had a... girlfriend who used to do that. Trichotillomania."

"Trick 'er tell 'er what?"

"You know, that, uh, compulsive disorder that women get. Mostly women. Where they, uh, pluck hairs out of their head."

"I never heard of that!"

"Yeah, really. My ex, she would just pull 'em out all the time from off the top of her head. She said she didn't feel anything. She said it felt kinda good. In any case, she couldn't help it. She was bald at the top of her head. She had to hide it, by like combing her regular hair over it."

"Geez. I guess that's kinda like me."

"Oh, well, not really. Not exactly." I move closer to her. "Your... thing doesn't show up in public. I mean, people can't see it, unless you show your toes."

"Sometimes I do it on my fingers too. But most people just think that since I work with my hands a lot, you know, it's no big deal. I don't do it too often on my fingers. I like my big... left... toe..." She says it so playfully, like a little girl. Ladies and gentlemen, José is aroused.

"Mm-hmm." Closer. She pretends not to notice.

"But it's true, you know. I'm like your ex. I don't really feel a thing. I mean, when I'm doing it, I see the blood, and the flesh tearing off, and I know in my mind I'm sticking a piece of metal deep into my skin — but I can't help it. I see the blood pumping out — sometimes it's really a lot before I stop myself and get a towel. Sometimes I do it in the tub. Like Marat. My blood is black in the tub. I know it's bad, but I keep doing it. Ever since I was a little girl. I can't help it. I'm like your ex. It does feel kinda good."

"Yeah."
"You're not listening to me, are you?"
"Mm-hm."
"What did I say?"
"Right now?"
"Mm-hm."
"You said, uh, that it feels kinda good."
"An' what else?"
"Ah, come on, don't make me say it all."
"You weren't paying attention. You just want to fuck me."
"Ahem. Um, you don't have to, uh, put it that way."
"I bet you do."

A pause. Eye to eye.

"I'm sorry," I say. Retreat. "I should've been paying attention."

We get ready to crash, she in her little standard issue Russian living room whose couch converts into a bed, me in the tiny kitchen on a cot. I feel self-conscious pulling my pants off —she can see me. We're barely ten yards from each other in her cramped little Soviet apartment. The denim slips from my hairy, jiggly white thighs and I slip under the covers, like a coy bride, feeling her eyes on me. Her unimpressed eyes.

"Good night, José," she says, a little dully, and I hear her sheets rustle.

"Uh, good night."

I fall asleep pretty fast, to the tick of the kitchen clock and the hiss of the gas stove, which she keeps on at a low level. I stare at the blue flame for a few seconds in the darkness, then turn over on to the surprisingly comfortable cot.

We say nothing else.

Morning. The sun shines full force in these Khrushchev-era highrise kitchens. It was part of the design for these "Khrushchevki": the maximalization of resources, like pointing the large kitchen window towards the sun or the other transomlike window that lets light shine into the adjacent WC. This way when you want to take a shit you only need to turn one light on instead of two. I wake up remarkably refreshed. Cynthia's moving about. The light has erased the sexual tension. My sexual tension.

"How'd you sleep?" she asks, washing some cups in her aluminum sink. She's wearing a gray T-shirt that comes down to her knees. Barefoot. Left toe wrapped in several layers of bandage.

"Fine." Her movements over the dishes are quick, matter of fact. The water splashes over her hands, the suds rise through her fingers. Still lying in bed, I note her olive calves. Then I remember something. "I dreamt… I dreamt about a dog. Barking at a spaceship, a rocket, that like shoots up into the air and…"

"A dog that what?" She turns to me as her hand reaches for the faucet. I hear the crinkle of cracked ceramic. "Oh, shit."

The cup has slipped, banged against the sink, perished. She's sucking her finger, cat-like.

"You okay?"

"Yeah. That old thing was so cracked it wasn't gonna last much longer anyway. Shit. Knicked my finger."

"Sorry 'bout that. At least you've got lots of bandages on hand."

She laughs, her hair in the sun. This, this sun-dappled clip, is my clearest, dearest image of her. "Yeah. You must think I'm a freak. A bleeding New York mama. Look." She walks up to me, shows me the finger. I sit up in the cot. "Look how black it is. Why is it so black?"

"You probably hit an artery, I guess. Lemme see. Oh, that's not so bad. It's better off than the cup."

She starts to pull her hand away, I hold it in place. I hold it up close, inspect her thin, 28-year-old digit, with the tiny gash at its tip. "Here's a 'hot spot' for you." Before I realize it, I kiss the little wound, a quick booboo peck. "You'll be alright."

"Thanks," she says, a little taken aback, returns her finger to her lips. The unexpected intimacy, for both of us, sort of hangs in the air for the slightest of seconds. She goes back to the living room. A minute later the stereo is on, an American English-language radio show, complete with moronic trivia and laugh tracks, comes on. They're discussing Michael Jackson's sex life, long after he left Moscow.

I'm just about done putting my clothes on when I hear her over the bimbo DJ's wail.

"Yo, listen, I don't want to rush you, but they're coming for me at 12 and I've still got a lot of packing and, you know, straightening out to do."

"Noo problem." I'm folding the cot. It doesn't cooperate.

"I warned you last night, right?" She's at the door, thin brown hair combed over one shoulder. "Oh, don't worry. I'll do that. Leave it."

"Only if you still respect me." I turn to her, sort of smile. I look like shit in the morning light.

"Huh?"

"You know. Respect me in the morning? Get it?"

"Whatever, José."

I'm being rushed and coaxed and not offered breakfast and politely sorta kicked out, in a friendly, even laughing way. She's forgotten the respect crack, thank God. She is back to being a cat: lithe, direct, invulnerable. Her thumb has a tiny band aid, the smallest one in the pack.

She opens the door, leads me down the dark hall with sunlight breaking through it in shafts from the window around a corner.

"You know how to get back to Vernadsky, right? Walk out, turn left, follow the building left past the bushes and you'll see it."

"Okay, Mom."

"Sorry to kick you out." We're waiting for the elevator, whose creaking reverberates through the hall. It won't be long.

"Hey, no problem. Thanks a lot for the cot. It was really comfy. And, hey, you know, about last night…"

The elevator doors open with a scrape and bounce.

"Don't worry about it." She seems a little annoyed that I brought it up.

"Just don't advertise my toe everywhere."

I put two fingers to my lips and smile, with my fat ugly face, my rotten hair, my pathetic wardrobe. I am no Denzel Washington. Cynthia goes for the hug before I do; she's much surer, much more controlled, than I. She feels thin and warm in my arms; I hold the elevator open with a foot. She smells of dishwashing liquid. As we part in the dark she brushes her lips against mine, the briefest, faintest, glancingest graze, that still scorches. There is wetness and heat and profundity in that unkiss, a Cheshire kiss, her mouth overloads mine with sensation. She grins as she steps back, the green in her eyes arching to yellow.

"Have a nice trip," I say, stepping in.

"Take care of yourself," she replies, with suddenly sleepy lids. It's an expression of warmth, her smile effortless, her arms crossed. The doors slide.

"See ya." They're the last words I hear her utter before the doors merge. She stands steadfast in the dark and drafty corridor that swallows her in its shadow as the doors creak shut.

Ten floors later, I'm standing outside the urine-soaked *podyezd* with the door on one hinge, in full painful sun. There is no one on the street, on the sidewalk, only parked cars. The trees sway in the gentlest of breezes, cool and Springlike.

I walk left, tasting putrid saliva in an unwashed mouth. My body soon unstiffens from its night's repose, the kinks in my knees resolve themselves into another day's service. And as I walk with my head bowed, avoiding the sharp glints off the cars, my mind wanders back to the dream I had last night.

A dog, and a rocket. And the dog is chasing the rocket as it zooms up into the white-blue sky, on a trail of spume. And the dog barks, I can't tell in anger or regret.

And the rocket explodes, way up in the middle of the air.

Like that. That way. That's what I mean. That way. I gotta piss again.

Yes, okay, yes, yes, okay, okay, yes, yes, yes, okay okay, yes, yes, okay, right, yes, yes, okay, right, right, right, yes, okay, be right with you, right, okay, yes, yes, yes, okay. *Da. Da. Da.*

I'm drunk.

A little.

Crowds, crowds. *Les foules. Toute le monde.* The ex-dinosaur girl is talking with Ms. Mammaries, who's getting her ass stroked by the old geezer. Is that a million roubles in your pocket, or are you just happy to see me?

Ah. Guess what. Paul Datum. And his *okhran*tourage. Despite what ensues, it must be understood that deep down inside I feel a great respect, in this era of crude accumulation of capital, for this sleazeball white trash entrepreneur who founded a hotel in Moscow — and who's now in the fight of his life to keep it from his turncoat Russian partners. The man is a Good American, who'll fight the good fight — too bad he's an asshole. (Crapulousness makes us crude.) All ex-pats know three things about Paul Datum: his embarrassing love of *Star Trek* videos; his unflinching business savvy; and his living on borrowed time.

He pops up out of nowhere ("José.") stops me with his palm on my chest ("José!"). Danke.

"Yo there, José. Easy. How ya doin'?" (He says it "Ho-say.")

"Fine, Paul. Fine." His bodyguards, too bull-necked crewcuts in Versace, give me the Clint Eastwood squintsky. "How's, uh, how's business?"

"I'll show you how's business." And Mr. Datum, captain of industry slingshooting it in the Wild East, pulls up close and opens his coat slightly — enough for me to see the kevlar vest, snug on his torso. So the legends are true. The Oklahoma Kid. "It's like I told ya in the interview. Other folks might run, but I'm here for the long haul. If they wanna fuck me, I'll fuck 'em back twice as hard. In their smallest hole, bud."

"My hero."

"What's that?"

"Been here long?"

"Nuh-uh. I ain't staying neither. Just wanted to make my appearance, to show these assholes they ain't dealin' with some chicken-shit small businessman. I ain't no band leader." (He really said that, reader.) "I made the Raduga what it is, and if I go it goes."

"Right."

"And just 'tween you an' me, I showed up 'cuz I fronted Clay and Shaw some startin' capital for this place. Cleared a couple'a hurdles for 'em, if you know what I mean." (He blinks in my face) "Just 'tween you an' me. Off the record."

"Right."

"Now how about that story, José? You told me a week, buddy. Y'all've been sittin' on that thing for damn near a month. Now I'm askin' ya, one southerner to another — you're from Texas, right? — the *Post's* gonna help me with this court fight or what? Publicity's what I need, good publicity, if'n you take my meaning. I gave you exclusive access to my holodeck, buddy. Now that's worth a front page, ain't it? I been here eight years, son, eight goddamn years, an' I ain't goin' nowhere. Now you help me out, I help you out. That's how it works. It ain't no secret your paper needs a hand… So c'mon, José — I got lotsa Mexican friends back in Oklahoma, by the way, great people, beautiful people, beautiful women — c'mon, let's get this sumbitch out to press, huh? An' I'll make it worth your trouble to take that extra step."

(is my eye wandering? hold me up, Paul)

"Look, no one cares about your piece 'a shit rag, but they read your stuff. You're about the only thing keeping that sucker from being totally worthless, all due respect to Anthony an' all. You ever get tired 'a the com-*Post,* you come an' work for me."

"Like Paul Nixon?"

"That's right. Like Paul. He wrote a few nice things about me an' now he's on my staff. He's on the payroll, an' it's a hell of a lot more glamorous than…"

"I ain't Paul, Paul. I ain't on your payroll and you can't give me orders. The story'll run this week — maybe — as a page 10 feature, like all my (hic) personality profiles. You're just gonna have to wait your turn, like e-e-e-everybody else."

Datum winces, possibly at my breath, possibly like a man in the dark who's just bumped up against a wall. I prefer the latter.

"Awright, amigo," he says, smiling, his shark eye darting, darting. "You take care a' yourself. I'll be watching out for that thing this week. Nice talkin' to ya."

"Pleasure. Send an away team, Number One."

"What was that?"

"See you. Stay clean. Have some fun."

Beam me up. Engage cloaking device. Eh kain't do it, keptin, the engine's is frozen and I need to throw up… no. No no. Okay, okay, yes, yes yes yes yes I'm okay I'm okay I'm okay *Da Da da…*

*DENIAL*BARGAININGDEPRESSIONACCEPTANCE

It's a blur. blur. It's a blur. The rest is silence. I remember nothing, absolutely nothing else at all. Wait a minute. There's tons more. I forgot I forgot.

"Miles, I'm not gon' compromise my journlistic effics. Don' ask me. Don' ask me."

"José, I'm telling you, man — whoops, you okay? I'm telling you, this is the first English language cinema in Moscow. You gotta give Datum credit for the balls it took to open it at the Raduga. Okay? I'm not taking anything away from that. As a lawyer, I admire the balls it took to even open that thing up in this fucking place. But the theater needs help, man. This is not for print. Is this your drink? This is off the record. The opening was great. *Much Ado,* politicians, champagne,

Datum: Weird Scenes Inside the Bunker

"Meet the man behind the headlines," read the invitation. "Escape the challenging schedule of sununit events."

Paul Datum had wanted to attract the world's atention for quite a while, so when the eyes and ears of the world landed literally in his backyard, he was ready.

He distributed dozens of the small flyers amongst media representatives covering the May 10 Gore/Chernomyrdin summit, who just happened to be assembled at the US Embassy's press centre on the second floor of the Hyatt-Raduga Hotel. It was a convenient elevator ride up to Datum's eighth-floor apartment, where the embattled president of Ameruss Business Centres had been holed up for weeks in a dispute with his Russian partners.

In fact, a platoon of bodyguards stationed in the room 24 hours a day was all that prevented those Russian partners from evicting Datum out of the hotel for alleged rent arrears.

But now, fate- and presidential politics — had handed him a proverbial golden opportunity.

"You are invited... to our hospitality suite," read Datum's announcement, which attracted several journalists, embassy staff, security guards and the merely curious to enjoy a copious buffet in the Oklahoman's living room.

"Come in! How are you? Would you please sign our guestbook?" Datum greeted one new guest. "Yeah, it's all free! There's good fresh doughnuts, fresh coffee, decaf," he added, like some parody of Special Agent Dale Cooper from Twin Peaks.

Besides the goodies, Datum had on hand several copies of a thick bound volume of Xeroxed articles pertaining to his case, the most high-profile example of a Moscow joint-venture gone bad. The volume's cover showed a familiar Ameruss ad, the well-known slogan "The Environment for Business Success in Moscow" stamped over with the word DECEASED in red letters.

Datum's summit ploy got results, including a front-page article in USA Today, stories in the International Herald Tribune business section and other periodicals, keeping the 40-year-old entrepeneur's troubles in the spotlight, bringing world scrutiny to his warnings of Russia's "creeping renationalisation" - a nice side show to the first "Cold Peace" summit.

A few weeks after his "hospitality suite" stunt, Datum, still entrenched in his room with round-the-clock protection, reflected on the idea.

"It was really successful," he said. "We got a lot of nice people interested in our problem, and that'll help us out."

Datum's problem, as has been widely reported, stems from Hyatt International and the Moscow City

Property Committee's attempts to drop him from their joint venture partnership for financial misdoings and unpaid back rent. Datum, who founded the hotel in 1990 and owns a 40 per cent stake in it, has accused his rivals of greed and lawlessness, claiming the disputed fees are covered by the original contract.

However, that contract may no longer apply after a series of renegotiations, so both sides have fired off suits and countersuits in various arbitration courts. The stalemate has kept Datum locked out of his office and in his three-room suite in a virtual siege environment since April. Fearing deportation — or worse — if he leaves the premises, Datum has taken to wearing a bullet-proof vest on the few occsasions when he ventures out of his room. The rest of the time, he's dug in, doing business by fax and cellullar phone from the bunker of room 850.

Still, for a bunker, it's not bad.

Once you knock on the door, you'll hear cries of "Dver!" ring from within — Datum or one of his assistants announcing to the guards there's someone who wants in. A guard will look you over and, satisfied, allow you past the threshhold into the living room.

This charmingly small chamber decorated with a large kite on the wall and a Calfornia flag draped over a door, sports a priceless view of the Moskva river with the Ministry of Foreign Affairs buiding behind. There's a TV, a stereo, CD's representing several different genres from jazz to New Age to country to 70s classic rock, a plaque of appreciation given to Datum by his employees, a *Star Trek* matryoshka set, a bookcase with books on Russian art, politics, how to become a "power speaker." Goods, including teas, vitamins, supplements and spirits almost spill over from the shelves.

Datum soon appears, dripping in a brightly coloured robe of vaguely native American design. "I've just been sweating out in my bathroom," he declares. Does he have a sauna in there? "No, no, I just turn the hot water up as high as it'll go, and sit there and just sweat."

Datum, with his infamous business style based on not letting others see him sweat, warms up for a short tour of his bunker. He goes on and on about the smallest trinket and detail, clearly enjoying the chance to show off his home, like the host of some *Lifestyles of the Rich and Besieged* programme.

After letting you peek into his "toys" drawer ("for when I have to entertain the little ones"), he leads you into his inner sanctum. A huge king-size bed dominates the room, with a large TV poised like a cannon before it. A Russian doll sits calmly atop the TV, as if it had climbed up there to enjoy the view of the various bric-a brac scattered throughout the chamber. The bathroom, still emitting steam, is off to the left.

"This is my Star Trek collection," Datum points to a shelves stacked to overflowing with videotapes, his pride and joy. "This is my classic Trek right here, and this over here is all Next Generation. I have a buddy taping Voyager for me in the States."

His favourite episode?

"The one where Picard turns into a Borg.

Lokutos. Yeah, that's it, Lokutos."

He'll lead you back to the living room, to sit down on a plush dark armchair for a chat. The frequent interruptions break the flow of conversation, but they also provide an interesting view into Datum's day-by-day existence — as well as his infamously imperious style.

"It has to have the letterhead on it," he barks at a secretary. "No, our letterhead. And as soon as you copy it, you fax it over to them. And not just a fax, you make a copy and send it over by car. Yes, by car! And I want it done PDQ, you understand? Now!"

Datum's polite, cheelful attitude towards his guest, contrasting with his sharp orders to underlings, only adds to the surreal atmosphere of this unique corporate den, with bodyguards walking to and fro, phones ringing, the TV blaring — and Datum at the centre of it all.

Which makes it hard to credit that up until his junior year of high school, Datum was "basically an introvert." An accident at 13 (he broke his hip while chasing the dog) exiled him to a hospital bed for two and a half months, while subsequent complications with kidney stones and surgery kept him bedridden at home for over half a year.

Even after recovery, a weak abdominal area area kept him from becoming a jock — a hard thing to live down in Oklahoma City — so he settled for "being a brain."

Still, this son of an insurance agent was dubbed "most likely to do the most interesting things, something like that," in his yearbook. In 1977, while a senior at Oklahoma State, he took part in the Semester at Sea programme, a sort of floating college that stops at several ports around the world. On board the S.S. Universe, Datum took classes in international marketing, but his greatest education came from the fantastic places he saw: Korea, Taiwan, Sri Lanka, India, Singapore, Tunisia, to name a few.

"I was shocked by the international cultural experience," he says, flatly. "I decided not to go back to school. I didn't want to. I didn't want to finish, I didn't need it, I'd gotten bored. After going around the world, college just wasn't what I wanted to do anymore."

Politics offered Datum the challenge he needed. An avid and capable fund raiser since high school, the 21-year-old had put together the money for his Semester at Sea ($10,000) in three weeks — a fact which greatly impressed the Oklahoma Republican party.

Within three years he had become a Republican Eagle, a title conferred on those who raise over $10,000 a year after taxes for the Republican cause. He was, in fact, the youngest Eagle in the country at the time.

"And I want it done PDQ, you understand? Now!"

Among other feathers in his cap, Datum sought to "bring Richard Nixon in from the cold" in 1978. He was part of a delegation of party officials who went to visit the disgraced former president in California to prod him back out into the limelight. It was just this sense of anything being possible, Datum says, that led to his fascination with and zest for politics.

"That's one of the things that has always excited me: a changing environment. A constant environment bores me, extremely... Structure seems confining."

After a stint in the Ronald Reagan presidential campaign in 1979-80, Datum got into the oil business and consulted with numerous companies. His talent for convincing people to invest — regardless of the advisability of such a move — served him well, and led to new projects.

In August, 1985 he formed part of the first American trade mission to Russia after Mikhail Gorbachev's rise to power. Representing several businesses under the banner SovAmerica Trading Company, Datum saw a government in the final stages of collapse due to faltering hard currency reserves.

Reagan foreign policy in the 80s, he explains, convinced the Saudis to glut the market and force the price of oil way down, imperiling the Soviet Union's ability to gain hard currency through export of its own oil. This strategy, along with outspending the USSR militarily, eventually caused the collapse of the USSR — but also had the unfortunate effect of destroying the oil business in the States.

Datum, who had made money in oil investment and real estate, suffered along with the USSR to the tune of over $1 mil in oil losses. But he was already thinking of leaving Oklahoma anyway — for Russia, and its untapped potential.

"I saw the opportunity was tremendous, but I also saw the difficulties. When it takes Honeywell eight months to open an office and get their phones turned on, something's wrong here...

"I thought, boy, just to start a business here would eat up a quarter of a million dollars a year. But I decided the way not to have that happen was to create a business where I provided those services to other people and could take advantage of the services myself, to create a business that I could be used to create other businesses. To make this, in effect an incubator. "

The Ameruss Business Centres, with its problem-solving secretaries, fax, phones, computers, and other services, was born. Datum brought together a group of investors (including Nixon's formerly jailed chief of staff H. R. Haldeman), Hyatt International and Intourist in 1990 to seal a joint venture deal, which gave Moscow the Hyatt-Slavyanskaya Hotel.

The idea was for Ameruss, based in California, to manage the business centre and several floors of offices in the hotel. That part has worked out fine, and the hotel has been turning over $50 mil in profits. But those huge profits, Datum says, are the root of the present day evils, which have led to angry denunciations, charges of discrimination against foreigners, bullet-proof vests, power drills and all sorts of other props that journalists delight to report on.

It has led to life in a bunker for Datum, the Oklahoma Kid determined to slug it out to the last. In the roiling sea of invective that is the Slavyanska battle, Datum is certainly not guiltless (accusations of impropriety and threatened lawsuits have dogged his US ventures over the last few years), but even his enemies grant the man some grudging admiration. After all, he's been able to hold off forces that have overwhelmed other foreign businessmen in this country.

"Look at the Irish House," he says, noting another in a trend of joint ventures fallen out of foreign hands. "Look at what's happening. I'm standing here all alone against this sort of thing. I've been here for six years, this is all I've got. I have to stand and fight."

Datum as noble knight on the frontiers of the capitalist "wild East"? Hardly. Even as he awaits decisions from arbitrations courts in Russia and Sweden, business proceeds as usual. From the comort of his bunker, Datum is developing a $115 mil deal with Hyatt Hotels for a venture in Nizhny Novgorod.

The whole Ameruss spectacle has not been without its self-promoting, guerilla theatre-style pizazz. But Datum, accused more than once of being a publicity hound, may wind up staying in his "hospitality bunker" until late summer or fall. But he's not sweating anymore.

"I'm here 'til this is over," he says, reclining comfortably on his couch. "You might say it's "til death do us part.'"

VITAL STATISTICS
Paul Datum
Position: President and CEO of Ameruss
Age: 40
Hails from: Oklahoma City, OK Sound Bite: "I can't wait to get out and fly my kites again"

---

packed house. Fine. They didn't deliver on Sean Leonard or whatever his name is, but fine. Nice party. Good press.

(—"Yeah, I saw it. It opened at the Ameruss House of Cinema couple'a weeks ago. Yeah, Denzel's, uh, hot."—)

"But, just between you and me, those people have their heads up their ass. They're mismanaging the fuck out of that place. You listening? Attendance is already going down, and this first month is critical. We gotta have the numbers to show the distributor. Or else that's it, buddy. The place closes, just like that. I don't give a fuck what Samantha and Tsaryov and those other assholes are tellin' you. The place is not delivering the goods, not like it needs to. And I'm just asking you, cuz people read your stuff, okay, you know, you could really help this thing. You can bring people in. A good review, good press from you guys and from the *Herald*... You know this is a small community we got here. If we want to have services like this, we gotta support the venues. Or it's gonna dry up, I'm telling you. This is a critical time, the beginning. In five years, we're talking megaplexes all down Tverskaya, I'm talking THX, popcorn, the whole nine yards. But it's all gotta start somewhere, an' this is it and we gotta support it. You can help it, buddy. Now all I'm asking is that you work with that in mind."

"Tha' secon' feature, *Gunmen*. It was a piece'a shit. An' that matinee, *Dark Horse*? Wha the ffffuck was that? The girl gets injured by a horse, an' then falls in love with it. Wha the fuck was that? I wrote whatta thought of 'em. *Tochka*."

"Look, man, that's what I'm saying. We can't be... I mean, they can't be promoting the fuck out of this thing, advertising in your papers, spending hard currency from the firm's own reserves, you know, and then the ads are right next to shitty panning reviews. I told that Covino asshole what the fuck are you doing? This goes way beyond your cutesy, smartass reviews, 'Look how shitty this movie is, look how clever I sound.' We can't get the good stuff right now because we gotta show the distributor we're for real. Now that Samantha bitch wants to bring in this fucking art film, this, uh, this, uh..."

"*The Plague*."

"Right. And we don't even know what it is. It hasn't opened anywhere, it's been gathering dust on some studio shelf for two years. I hear it's a downer. Who the fuck in Moscow is gonna want to go see a fucking depressing movie?"

"Camus."

"Canoe?"

"Camus. The author. It's based…"

"Yeah, yeah, whatever. Look, okay, I know you think these action films were shitty, but it's what the marketing says we need. This is a tough sell, man, with this video piracy and instability and shit. We gotta pay extra for security. The fucking print comes with a bodyguard! We gotta put this fat asshole up, feed him, get his dick sucked, keep the print overnight in the safe, all at Golden Ring expense, okay? Just so we can get the damn thing. Okay? That's the environment we're dealing with here. You guys have gotta help us. Or it's all gonna go under, just like that. I'm just thinking about the ex-pat community here, is all…"

"C'mon, Miles. I'm drunk, I'm not stupid. You're playing both angles on this deal, an' you know it. No more for me, thanks. Maybe some water. Never mind. (hic) Look, you've got your little investment deal with Datum, you've got your interest in the local distributor, what's it called, Golden Ass?"

"Golden Ring."

"Right. Golden Ass. An' then you've got your fucking Samson, David & Goliath, attorneys at law, consultin' on the whole thing. So my heart is really bleed… um, um, s'cuse me."

DENIAL*BARGAINING*DEPRESSIONACCEPTANCE

issy poo, pissy poo, I love you, come out, come out wherever you are, oh, I pray thee, gentle mortal, sing again I'm okay you're okay okaaaay, piss it out, piss it owwwwt, Roy, Roy, Ro-O-O-O-O-oy, whoo, never again, never again, I promise, I pretty promise, I oops! a little on the leg, okay okay okay, hey, buddy, I hear it's open bar tonight, this bath, oops, r-r-r-r-r, this bathroom looks looks looks like a tomb, Vladimir Ulyanov, it's tomb to go, we can't preserve the past, even in formaldehyde, no more for me thanks, What's that? … Right… Dmitrevskoye… near the railway station… "It'll take a few moments to get the coordinates from the navi-computer." "Are you kidding? At the rate they're gaining?" "Traveling through hyperspace ain't like dusting crops, boy…" Mmm. Mmmmmmm.

Urethra Franklin. Ellen, you missed a good one. Gucci wire rim this… and by that I don't mean the mafia, zip zip zip, o-o-oh, gastric juices, entrails, Reverend Runt, what time might it be? Mistress, it is…

"Khasé? That is you, isn't it? Are you well, my friend?"

"Yura. Yuuuuuuurechka. I and my member here were just to... having been performed a hallucination of you. A hallucination of you with you in it. Hallucination about you."

"I understand, I understand, my friend. I believe you failed to follow my advice. You should leave the real drinking for those nationally disposed (?) to it. You are (untranslatable). But you're still standing, and where there's life there's hope. And where there's death there's work. Come on outside."

"Never again, Yurechka, eh?"

"Right, my friend, right. By the way, I saw you talking to that walking corpse, Datum. He is not long for this world (?), believe me. Perhaps another ten months and then KRRK! I would advise you not to hang around him, unless you like the idea of turning your brains into swiss cheese. Speaking of brains, I wrote something last month on this poor bastard, a man from the Yugo-Zapadnaya district. They bashed his head in with a wrench. (?) They left his body in the courtyard of some korpusy, his head hanging out of a dumpster. By the time the cops fished him out the rats and stray dogs had had all night to feast (?) on his brains. They licked the inside of his skull clean. You see, brains are like yogurt. They..."

"Khasé, are you alright?... ... Get to the metro. You have 30 minutes. Just go straight there and drink some water before you go to bed. You'll be fine. I see that I must go. This Yid bastard is finally flying the coop (?)."

"One other thing. This parliament business. It's much worse than even I thought. Be very careful, Khasé. Be careful you don't get washed away along with the garbage. It would be best for you to leave the country for a time, I think. Take your vacation. Something big is coming down, possibly as soon as a couple of weeks. My sources are very nervous, though others, of course, welcome the upsurge (?) in business. This will be..."

"yrrr uzhhrr vzylllsvrrknkrrli vprrrshlmmmztstsmm"

"What?"

"I... I am alrrrdy takin' my va-kay-shun last month."

"I see. Well, get going, my friend. Get to the metro. I too must fly. Poka."

I turn to Tim. No, wait. No, I don't.

A bigger blur. A huger blur. Bright. Something's cooking. Bubble, bubble, toilet trouble. The Planet Manhattan kitchen. What the hell am I doing in here? A bunch of the flown-in types, a couple of hot models. Are they… oh, my God, yes. They're snorting coke. The *Village Voice* guy, too. My, my. How McInerney. This really is a New Yawk club. They're trying out its sea legs. Open the pod bay doors, Hal. Geez. This is too banal, really, and I'm too drunk, too whatever, to try to be anymore clever. I give up. I'm really not even thinking these words, these thoughts, I'm really not sentient in the normal sense. I am only a shapeless sponge of sensation.

Thas okay. Hmm. Some people making out on the sleek metal table. Me? My name's José. Dolph Lundgren. The guy talking to me — mmeeeeeee? — looks like Dolph Lundgren, same spiked hair, same tall, lean body. A white smelly leather jacket. His lips are moving, he's smiling, smug, it's all just pops an' whistles to me. The architect? Holy shit, this is the architect. This is his place. Ha ha ha ha ha ha. Finger dips into his breast pocket, voilà, a business card. He puts it in *my* breast pocket. I'm outta here.

DENIALBARGAINING*DEPRESSION*ACCEPTANCE

over, all over, over heeeeeeeeeeeeeeaave oh, oh, oh,
heeeeeeeeeeeeeeeeeeeeeave gah, gah, gah, oooooooooooh hkh hkh hkh hkk n n n n n heeeeeeeeeeeeeeeeeeeeeave hr rhrrhhhhhr rhrrnrk rhrrh (this is, um, well, yeah.)
hrrrrrrrrr hrrrrrrrrrkh kkh kh hrrrrrrrr, rp rop rp rp hurrrrrrrrrrrrrkh shpt shpt oh, oh, oh,
mmm ssssrrrr-rrhh rrr klllld uuuuuuuurr mmmt mmmmtlrffff jkkkkkkkk haaaaaaaaaaakhsakjhffjkhhhhhheeeeeeeeeeeeeeeeeeeeeeeeeeeeeeave
kh kh
kh kh kh kh heeeeeeeevrrrrrrrrrheeeeeeeeeeeeeeeeee****
****

"Well, well, look what we got here."
 "I told you this one was trouble. Asiatics. Look at this asshole. Get up. Get up. Fuck, he's covered in it. Come on."
 "Get up, time to go home. Get up, you shit."
  mrrrrrrrrrkh gah gah mrrrkh
 "Come on, come on. Out. I oughta stick your face in it, you whoreson." (?)
 "Fuck. Fuck. Who do you think is gonna clean this? Look at that, the ceramic's all

covered in it. Fuck. Come on. Nooo, you're not pissing in this bathroom again. Piss in your pants, you fat fuck."

"Come on. Come on, I said."

mrrr bg mr bg mr bg

"Yeah, yeah, out we go."

mrr bg! mrrr bg! mrrr bgg!

"His bag."

"What?"

"His bag. You have a bag, dickhead?"

mr bg mrrr bg

"Yeah, it's a ticket here. Go get your fucking bag."

"Hurry up."

DENIALBARGAININGDEPRESSION*ACCEPTANCE*

cold. cold bridge. windy bridge. lonely bridge. moskva. *reka moskva.* moscow river. lonely cold windy bridge over moscow river.

money. money. taxi. metro closed closed. closed. closed. money taxi home metro closed. cold. cold bridge. windy bridge. lonely bridge. moskva. reka moskva. moscow river. cold lonely windy bridge over moscow river.

100. 100. 100. no change. no change. no good no good. rob. rob. money. money. taxi. metro closed closed. closed. closed. money taxi home metro closed. cold.

cold bridge. windy bridge. lonely bridge. moskva. *reka moskva.* moscow river. cold lonely windy bridge over moscow river.

shot. far. scream. echowalls. kremlin. sound. sound. unseen. home home home. where there's death there's work. 100. 100. 100. no change. no change. no good no good. rob. rob. money. money. taxi. metro closed closed. closed. closed. money taxi home metro closed. cold. cold bridge. windy bridge. lonely bridge. moskva. *reka moskva.* moscow river. cold lonely windy bridge over moscow river.

sleep. shot. far. scream. echowalls. kremlin. sound. sound. unseen. home home home. where there's death there's work. 100. 100. 100. no change. no change. no good no good. rob. rob. money. money. taxi. metro closed closed. closed. closed. money taxi home metro closed. cold. cold bridge. windy bridge.

lonely bridge. moskva. *reka moskva*. moscow river. cold lonely windy bridge over moscow river.

    no vacancy. rossiya. no vacancy. "sorry." kempinski. no vacancy. fuck you fuck you fuck you. sleep. shot. far. scream. echowalls. kremlin. sound. sound. unseen. home home home. where there's death there's work. 100. 100. 100. no change. no change. no good no good. rob. rob. money. money. taxi. metro closed closed. closed. closed. money taxi home metro closed. cold. cold bridge. windy bridge. lonely bridge. moskva. *reka moskva*. moscow river. cold lonely windy bridge over moscow river.

    ?? hello? no. shhhhhh. bag. mine. mine mine mine. shhh. no one. no one. steps. time? time? time? very cold. no vacancy. rossiya. no vacancy. "sorry." kempinski. no vacancy. fuck you fuck you fuck you. sleep. shot. far. scream. echowalls. kremlin. sound. sound. unseen. home home home. where there's death there's work. 100. 100. 100. no change. no change. no good no good. rob. rob. money. money. taxi. metro closed closed. closed. closed. money taxi home metro closed. cold. cold bridge. windy bridge. lonely bridge. moskva. *reka moskva*. moscow river. cold lonely windy bridge over moscow river.

    up. up. upsy daisy. no. no. no. hrrrrrrk hrrrrrk. heeeeeeeeeeave. no. no. cold co-O-O-O-O-old. fr fre free freez freeze. d d d d d… ?? hello? no. shhhhhh. bag. mine. mine mine mine. shhh. no one. no one. steps. time? time? time? very cold. no vacancy. rossiya. no vacancy. "sorry." kempinski. no vacancy. fuck you fuck you fuck you. sleep. shot. far. scream. echowalls. kremlin. sound. sound. unseen. home home home. where there's death there's work. 100. 100. 100. no change. no change. no good no good. rob. rob. money. money. taxi. metro closed closed. closed. closed. money taxi home metro closed. cold. cold bridge. windy bridge. lonely bridge. moskva. *reka moskva*. moscow river. cold lonely windy bridge over moscow river.

la cucaracha

la cucaracha

ya no puede caminar

porque no tiene

porque le falta

marijuana que fumar

going going. arriba arriba ándale ándale. ouch. ouch. ouch. ouch. ouch. ouch. up. up. upsy daisy. no. no. no. hrrrrrk hrrrrk. heeeeeeeeeeave. no. no. cold co-O-O-O-O-old. fr fre free freez freeze. d d d d d... ?? hello? no. shhhhhh. bag. mine. mine mine mine. shhh. no one. no one. steps. time? time? time? very cold. no vacancy. rossiya. no vacancy. "sorry." kempinski. no vacancy. fuck you fuck you fuck you. sleep. shot. far. scream. echowalls. kremlin. sound. sound. unseen. home home home. where there's death there's work. 100. 100. 100. no change. no change. no good no good. rob. rob. money. money. taxi. metro closed closed. closed. closed. money taxi home metro closed. cold. cold bridge. windy bridge. lonely bridge. moskva. *reka moskva*. moscow river. cold lonely windy bridge over moscow river.

going going. arriba arriba ándale ándale. ouch. ouch. ouch. ouch. ouch. ouch. up. up. upsy daisy. no. no. no. hrrrrrk hrrrrk. heeeeeeeeeeave. no. no. cold co-O-O-O-O-old. fr fre free freez freeze. d d d d d... ?? hello? no. shhhhhh. bag. mine. mine mine mine. shhh. no one. no one. steps. time? time? time? very cold. no vacancy. rossiya. no vacancy. "sorry." kempinski. no vacancy. fuck you fuck you fuck you. sleep. shot. far. scream. echowalls. kremlin. sound. sound. unseen. home home home. where there's death there's work. 100. 100. 100. no change. no change. no good no good. rob. rob. money. money. taxi. metro closed closed. closed. closed. money taxi home metro closed. cold. cold bridge. windy bridge. lonely bridge. moskva. *reka moskva*. moscow river. cold lonely windy bridgego. go. go. go. go. go. go. go. ouch. ouch. ouch. couch. couch. couch. couch. ouch

****** *****

the metro.
morning.
gettin' there.
rub a dub dub.

eyes. eyes.
rocking train.
vomit on chin.
izvinite.
sorry.

untranslatable. untranslatable.
(an old man? a bath robe? slippers? a halo?)
and so on and so forth.

trudge, trudge, trudge. the Yugo-Zapadnaya district. home. home. home.
a last detail: the neighbors downstairs, Cambodians, are cooking for the lunch crowd that comes to their restaurant-apartment. The smell is unearthly, creamy and venomous.
door.
bed.
home.

2.
ДВА

JIM WONDERBREAD CALLS the next morning, and God knows how the hell I manage to get up and answer.

"Hey, José." (Moscow phone crackle. You can hear other people talking on the same line, as if through paper walls fifty feet away)

"jim"

"I can hardly hear you."

"can't talk"

"Oh, okay. Listen, I'm calling from over here at the *Post*. Since you haven't come in yet, I wanted to know what we're doing with this Planet Manhattan opening. We're writing it together, remember? Well, it's getting towards four now and I thought we should discuss it..."

"'ere were you lass night?"

"Oh, I was there. Yeah, it was pretty fun. Funny how I never saw you. You went, right? Yeah, that's funny. I saw Vova and he said he'd seen you. Yeah. Funny."

I give Jim some rough details of the story, mostly off the top of my head, tell him to write it with or without my by-line. He says some very weird offbeat stuff, something that would only happen when I'm in this condition. I beg off and hang up. Not right now, Jim. The story comes out later, buried on the business page, my suggestions warped into bizarre trite phrases and total untruths. Right. Head split open, rats licking my yogurt. I crawl back into my dumpster and wait for the cops to fish me out.

And this concludes our broadcast day, all five minutes of it, for Sept. 20th, 1993. Static.

I will now attempt to paint a sketch of the next week

First of all, the set-up. I wake up on September 21, still feeling supremely poisoned, and somehow miraculously drag myself to work. I still cannot put anything in my mouth without gagging.

After the usual crowded commute, I walk in to our offices on the 6th floor of a Soviet-era foreigners' apartment complex near Gagarin Square. Danny, Cleveland's finest, meets me at the door, an unusual expression on his face — bemused trepidation, I'd call it — and says, "Hey, José, have you heard?"

A sinking feeling. We've been waiting for this.

"They're closing down the paper," I sigh.

"No, no," Danny answers, sports wire print-outs dangling from his hands like Santa's list. "Nothing like that. Yeltsin dissolved the parliament."

"No shit."

(This exchange recalls other, very similar conversations that I have with Danny at the door. Like eight months later. Again he meets me as I'm coming, long paper strips spilling out of his hands, the same nervous smirk.

"Hey José, have you heard?"

"They closed down the paper."

"No, nothing like that. Kurt Cobain died."

"No shit.")

So much for September 21. From that point this nasty political instability grips the country — or I should say, grips the immediate neighborhood of the impressive parliament building near the Arbat district.

It comes down, basically, to a personality clash between, on the one hand, a Mr. Yeltsin, president of the Russian Federation (who I understand has had his own nights of excess, though he doubtless did not them sleep off on a cold, lonely, windy bridge) and on the other, Mr's. Khasbulatov, Speaker of Parliament, and Rutskoi, exVice President, and their followers. To make a long story short, Yeltsin tires of their shit, and says the party's over. He tells the guests to get the hell out.

But the guests won't leave, saying it's their party now, and shack up in the apartment with the keg, i.e. the parliament building, aka the White House. Yeltsin stops the tap, turns out the lights, tells 'em I'm-a warnin' ya. He calls the cops and they bullhorn the apartment, "Come out with your hands up and no one gets hurt!" The rowdy boys inside stick their hands out the window from under the blind, flip 'em el birdo. Some of them moon the cops. The cops barricade the place with a ring of flunkies in riot gear. The parliament's friends come out of the woodwork, flood down to the White House — and then all *ad* breaks lose.

Major political crisis! Unrest in mother Russia! The foreign journalists love it. On with the show.

After that it's a smudgy blur. On Wednesday, I think, Cynthia calls me at the office. She wants to know what happened to me the night of the Planet Manhattan fiasco. She thought we'd agreed to meet and we'd walk together to the metro. She said she'd be right back to the table. She looked and looked and couldn't find me.

Where was I? This is something I cannot and never will be able to answer. Hell, that's where I was.

Another call comes from Datum; the secretaries don't get the message in time that *I'm not here*. He gets his lousy article, in the middle of everything else going on in the capital.

3.
ТРИ

The Moscow Tribune

MOSCOW, TUESDAY, OCTOBER 5, 1993

White House Falls to Yeltsin's Force
Fighting Continues; Curfew Imposed in City

By Jose Alaniz and Maria Korolov
The Moscow Tribune

All began to rustle, awake, burst into song, to make noise, to speak. Large drops of dew sparkled everywhere with diamond-like rays; the tolling of a bell, pure and clear as if it too were cleansed by the morning damp, greeted me from the direction I was walking, and suddenly, right beside me, driven by the boys I'd gotten to know, a rested herd rushed by...

–Ivan Turgenev, A Sportsman's Sketches

*If you want someone to blame/
Throw a rock in the air you're bound to hit someone guilty*

–U2, Dirty Day

MONTHS LATER, I WOULD still distinctly remember that the day before I had put on my olive drab army underwear. Standard issue, Ft. Jackson, South Carolina. Basic training. Summer, 1986.

They say Army underwear fits extra snug, so if you shit your pants under fire it won't fall out and trip you up while you're running away. Actually, I made that up. But it doesn't mean they don't say it. The point being that it might as well be true.

Of course, there was no way to know that I would not be coming home that night — or the next, or the next. Like Vaclav Havel, I'd have to hold my shit in 'til the worst was over. As I wrote for publication with my sensationalist purple pen, "It would be just me and my stained armed forces briefs against the year's scariest 48 hours." Ugh. But what the hell. It was a lede.

And as we say at the Post: if it bleedskis, it leadskis.

The Old Arbat. The mammoth gangsterscape of the Prague restaurant at one end, the city's third McDonald's at the other. The prettiest, most European walking arcade in Moscow sandwiched in between. October 2.

I smell the smoke before I see the plume of gray wafting in the air. The whole section near Smolensky metro is closed off. Protesters. Parliament supporters.

They want the barricades torn down. They have a right to meet with their elected representatives. Yeltsin has gone too far. Down with Yeltsin. Boris Nikolayevich Klinton.

These people are pissed off. I know. I was there. Talking to them during the barricade scuffles earlier in the week, the old, the angry, the shriveled and the desperate. And the insane. For the first time in my career as a journalist, I actually fear for my safety. They call us pigs, Zionists, media scum. These people have sticks in their hands. Rumors place the number of arms stockpiled in the White House as sufficient to supply an army for an extended siege. The deputies have been holed up in there for nine days, waving guns, inciting. They hate us.

The barricades.Wind, freezing rain.

"Why are you both here?" I ask Sergei and Volodya, the *Post's* two staff photographers.

"Fascists!" screams the crowd, a bubbling cauldron.

"Well, there's two of us," says Sergei, with ye standard sheepish grin. *"That way, if they kill one, there's a spare to take his place."*

A week later, the cauldron boils over. Shit. From the police cordon right where Kalininsky Prospekt meets the Golden Ring Road you can plainly see the smoking bonfire of junk: benches, tires, pieces of tenement. The men straddle their Commune-like fortifications like Hugo characters, waving their fists, their clubs, tossing stones. We all watch, more bemused than anything else. There are tourists walking by, asking if this is part of the Arbat's 400th anniversary celebrations (a curious coincidence).

One of our editors, the oh-so-British Deliah, tells me this is quite a jolly good show, isn't it? (She really said that: "a jolly good show.") All I see are ants, livid ants, crawling over their formicary, on the warpath. I will have cause to invoke the ant metaphor again. The cops are doing nothing.

They stand back and watch, keep the crowd behind the lines. Loyalties divided, everywhere, everywhere in this schizoid country.

"Why, Lord? Why? Why do you punish me, lord?"

The old woman hugs the trunk of a tree, pleads upwards to heaven. The barricade crowd, mostly pension-age, has been driven back 40 meters with truncheons and kicks. *"Why do you punish me so? I've suffered and suffered for so so long. Why? Why? Why?"*

The scene is perfectly framed. (Journalists are allowed to stay.) The woman in the foreground, with the features of a flogged pig streaming, streaming tears, her arms around a tree like it was God almighty. The cold drizzle cascades onto her face. Behind her, to the left about ten meters, two dog soldiers take a cig break. Their helmets tipped at — I believe the phrase is — a "rakish angle," they watch the woman and guffaw.

"Move your ugly ass from there, you old cunt. Once I finish this I'm going to bash your asshole in."

"Leave her alone. She's a virgin, can't you see?"

Yuk yuk yuk yuk.

"Why, Lord? Why? Why? Why?"

I walk away. I want to stop up my ears. I walk away, to a spot under a tree, with my Danish TV news colleagues, whose cameras point the other way.

I don't include this episode in my reporting.

Evening, October 3. Sunday. The *Post* office. CNN carrying frequent, not quite live, not quite continuous yet, coverage of — as they call it — "the unfolding events in Moscow." The TV blares in the corner while I work on stuff for the coming week, as is my habit. Feature: an avant garde documentarian who is also a martial arts expert and likes to make films with lots of gory surgery footage. He looks like Maxim Gorky on steroids. The past week's alcohol binge is but a bad memory. About 5 p.m.

BOOM.

We have a dramatic new development in our coverage of the Moscow unrest. We go now live to Claire Shipman in CNN's Moscow bureau…

Pouring. They're pouring, oozing, flowing in waves over the barricades. The buzz-saw concertina wire, the dog soldiers, the metal shields, the vehicles that form a ring around the White House. They are pouring through it, ripping their clothes on the wire, overwhelming the troops, who fire in the air then disappear in a sea of flailing fists and clubs. Some drop their weapons and run. Thousands. Thousands of them. Impossible to say if they're coordinated or not; they're just pouring through, breaking the barricade down, pummeling soldiers, stealing the shields, climbing in the trucks and playing bumper car with the government defenses.

Live, on CNN. An angry ant army, smoked out of its den, marching in chaos to its white mother hive — fuck the mixed metaphors, this is really happening.

Live. The roused ants, stinging, stinging, screaming, washing in ripples over the bridge. Shit, I was just on that corner yesterday. Oh, fuck The tourists. Oh, Jesus.

On. Retreating troops. A bloodied helmet on the head of an exultant babushka.

C. Barriers gone, demolished. Yeltsin out of town playing quarters at his dacha.

N. Through to the White House, a raging ant hill kicked too many times.

N. Night falls on Moscow. Rutskoi works up the mob from a White House balcony. *"We must take Ostankino! We must take the television tower!"* UUUR-RAAAAAH!

As it turns out, I'm the only one in the office, the only weirdo who works on weekends. Are we coming out tomorrow? Is there gonna be a special edition? How come nobody's calling? What do I do? I've only slept one night in my new apartment, in a room across from old, crotchety Vera Dimentievna. Hell, she's the kind of die-hard old guard matron who's out there setting cars on fire. Unless *Santa Barbara's* on tonight, that is…

Will I ever see my stuff again? Will I ever get home? Fuck me…

In burst Jim and Lee, the Wonderbread Twins. So called for their thorough, unreconstructed Midwestern blandness. Nicest, squarest guys you'll ever meet.

"We're lucky to be alive! They were yelling 'Yankee Go Home!' They tore down the pictures on the walls of the embassy compound! We were swallowed up by the mob! Some guy was shooting a machine gun right next us! TAT-TAT-TAT-TAT TAT! We almost bought it, José!"

Night. Rumors of tanks, the nearby Tula division, on the main road to the city. Yeltsin flies in on his helicopter, lands inside the Kremlin. A beautiful dolly shot of him as he strides, grim and heavy in a black overcoat, into his chambers. Kudos to the TV cameraman.

I call Cynthia. I want to talk. Maybe she'd like to go see a Denzel Washington movie tonight? And pizza afterwards? No answer. Nothing.

Call Lev Lvovich. Professional cynic. Drinking buddy. His wife answers, says he's coming. I wait ten minutes. The line remains open, but nobody comes.

Oooh, bad feeling. Bad feeling tonight. Gunfire at the Ostankino tower. Casualties. Tracer bullets like assassin Christmas lights. Yuri's gonna rake it in.

Then, we hear the rumble. An earthquake. The water in the cups ripples. We're on the sixth floor. We rush outside. The tanks. A convoy. Thundering down Leninsky Prospekt towards the center of the city. The streetlamps shine eerie and funereal on an endless stream of ordnance. Everything flashing by in patches, one surreal tableau after another. It's on.

"Hey José, we thought you might be there. Say, we're thinking of hooking up with David and Megan, going to check out Tverskaya. We hear there's a big rally of Yeltsin supporters massing at the Mossoviet." (The Moscow City Council building, across from the statue of Yuri Dolgoruky.) "Yes, I'm serious. Come on! Yeah! We're gonna hook up with 'em by the Pizza Hut, if that area hasn't been closed off yet. That's pretty close to Manezh Square and the Kremlin, of course. Oh, come on. Nothing's gonna happen. It's the safest place to be tonight. It's full of Yeltsinites. The good guys. Seriously, they're on channel 11, did you see that? They're broadcasting from there, telling people to come and show support for the president. Gaidar and Yavlinsky, a bunch of other people. Look, we're not going to fucking Ostankino. Yeah, I heard. They took the Mayor's building. Or, at least several floors of it. Man, this is pretty exciting shit, huh? Aw, come on, don't be a pussy. I thought you wanted to be John Reed. John Reed didn't watch things on CNN. Well, hey, the Kremlin's not the worst place to be buried, is it? Come on, this is once in a lifetime. We missed the '91 putsch, so now's our chance. Historical tourism or something, you could call it. Just take a... just take a taxi. Yeah. No, no. There's traffic, I can see it from my window. Get your ass in gear, boyo. We're gonna go honk if you love Yeltsin. And, hey, José? If you can find one, bring a gun."

I crash at Megan and David's, near Mayakovskaya Square. Three in the morning. On the living room couch, right next to their antique piano. I guess these Yale grads get all the good apartments, and in the center, too. I call Roy from their phone fax. He hadn't heard about the trouble here. He let my cat get run over.

Killed. O-o-o-h, just what I want to hear right now. Around five thirty I awake to the sound of Megan being interviewed over the phone by her local hometown TV news.

"It seems calm right now. We heard gunfire throughout the night, but not nearby. We're about a mile from the Kremlin here. Yes. It's calm and quiet in a very beautiful dawn here in Moscow…"

She's right. The daybreak really is gorgeous, the most beautiful I've ever seen — "crystal colours almost audible with beauty," I write for publication. "Bottomless blue sky. Was it the crystal clarity of the moment, the closeness of the angel of death, flapping its wings so near, on a day that promised more blood, guaranteed it — is that what made it so beautiful?" Oh, go fuck yourself.

From their 13th floor kitchen window, I look down and see two armored personnel carriers barreling down the street. They're the only traffic.

The dirty day is born.

The metros running as normal. Soon I'm back at the office, which buzzes alive with that mad brand of activity, at that unmistakable pitch, unique to newspaper staffs.

Anthony, known for leading by designating, skips his lieutenants and calls a full staff meeting. Usually he only gets us all together like this to tell us we have to take another pay cut, but today is different. Obviously. Today sweaty, flabby, Oedipal Anthony wants to prove that the lowly com-*Post*… sorry, I mean the *Moscow Post* can kick the snooty *Moscow Herald's* ass. Sorry, I mean *Moscow Hurl's* ass. Hell of a day.

"We will put out our finest edition ever tomorrow. We will show our advertisers that we are in this game for real. No more snide remarks about our misspelled headlines, imaginary stories, all that rubbish." (He really said "all that rubbish.") "I own this paper and I will see it take its rightful place in this market, one dead baby at a time if I have to." (That too.)

"José, Simon, Maria. You're point. You will go down to the White House — what's left of it —and get me the best goddamn coverage this paper has ever seen. They started bombing the building at 9:14, 30 minutes ago, from the Novoarbatsky Bridge. Those tanks are not letting up their shelling. I figure we have maybe three more hours before either a formal surrender — or an all-out assault on the parliament building. Those fanatics may have a death wish, but their ammo won't last forever. Maria already got us some hot exclusive reporting from the Ostankino firefight last night. Lucky for us you were in town. Now I want color pieces, background, a chronology, and from you three — the real story, on the streets. Got it?"

"Uh, Anthony," I venture. "Do you really need me for this? Don't you think it would be better for me to stay here and write the trunk story, coordinate the dispatches? That's what we do with elections. I've already been down to Tverskaya last night..."

"I want you there. I want your writing to be from real life. I want you to crank out the best goddamn piece of journalism you've ever written. You have to be there first-hand for that."

"But Anthony... it's dangerous. Simon has a family. He doesn't need to be there either."

"I'll speak for myself, José."

"Sorry. But I mean, all I'm saying is that we're essentially a small town newspaper; we publish this thing for a community of what, 14,000 English-reading ex-pats, give or take? The wire services have got real reporters out there, Anthony. Experienced people, stringers, like Maria. Hot spot types. People who cover firefights for a living. People who know what to do in these situations. I mean, are you just gonna send us out there with a notepad against bullets and grenades...?"

"This is not a debate. You get out there or you can pack your things and go right now. I'm trying to run a legitimate news organization here. This one story is worth a thousand of your movie reviews or 'Mexican food' columns. You get your ass out there and bring me back Khasbulatov's fucking head on a pike — or else...!"

Etc., etc.

The three of us set out to work. Hi-ho, hi-ho. The taxis are charging quadruple the usual rate to get us to the White House. We go from the flickering, 12-inch image on Anthony's satellite television screen to its big brother version, magnified a trillion times, blown up with 180 degree enhanced smellorama. Soon we're there, among the crowds come to watch the gladiatorial games.

The three stooges. Maria, a veteran of several Caucasus flare-ups. She lives for this shit. She, you know, loves the smell of napalm in the morning. That sort of thing. Simon, an Armenian who's seen his share of war back home. "I want to see these bastards burn, José. I want to see these backward communist retards get what they deserve. Yeltsin's no saint, but these people want to drag everybody back to a decade ago. Fuck that. You can't understand. You're a foreigner. These criminals want to make Armenians a subjugated people again. Before that day comes, I'll see their entrails spilled on the pavement and dance on their fucking graves." O-o-okey doke. And me. Ex-Army reservist. Served in support. In the rear, with the gear. Only fire I've ever been under was on a shooting range. My underwear is fastened to prevent accidents.

Smell that ozone from the weapons. Hear the ZZZZZZ of bullets overhead. It's child's play to *amerikansky korrespondent!!* our way past the troops sort of holding the crowd back. Soon they give up on the crowd control idea altogether, and people are free to roam as close to the action as they dare.

Simon and I wait, just within a hundred meters from the no-longer-White House, taking cover behind a downed gas truck. ZZZZZZZ. ZZZZZZZ. Maria, who looks comically gonzo in her photog's vest, frizzy hair and sunglasses, edges closer to the action. We lose her. There are bodies, heaps of meat and rags, lying here and there on the street, increasing in number and damage the closer they are to the building. I witness some supreme acts of bravery. Ambulance workers, Red Cross people, concerned friends, whatever they are, dashing out to the street in the open to pick up their felled comrades, to drag them away to safety if they can't walk. Big mushrooms of dust erupt all around them. Some don't make it back. Goddammit! Those are civilians! What are you maniacs doing?

Simon is interviewing some man who says he escaped from the other side. A couple of bearded shirtless potbellies right next to me are discussing the battle, downing malt liquor and laughing. Their teeth twist my stomach, and it's already in knots, thank you very much.

I content myself with "local color" observation, from well behind the truck.

Yeah, right, Anthony. This is gonna be the story of a lifetime, the best damn piece of journalism I've ever written. I'll fax it to you from the morgue.

"These people are crazy," says Maria, scaring the shit out of me. She suddenly pops up from the other side of the truck, leans back against it next to me. "This whole thing is crazy. I've been in the shit more times than I can count. That doesn't bother me. But in a real war, you know more or less where the bullets are coming from. I mean, the rules are sick rules, but they're rules, you know? These people are out of their minds. The whole fucking world is the enemy to them. They're firing whichever way they want. Two kids were gunned down right in front of me! José, this is the most dangerous thing I've ever done."

"... Thanks for the comforting words, Maria. Say, uh, do you think this truck is safe? What if it, like, uh, still has gas in it or something?"

"Oh, it does. Can't you smell it?"

"Oh."

"Don't worry. You're more likely to get a bullet in your torso. But we're pretty out of range here. They'd have to get a lucky shot. Unless, of course, they start using those M-60s again. And bazookas. I heard somebody had smuggled in..."

"That's fine, thank you. Fine. Save it for the article."

"You'll be okay, sweetheart."

She flashes her loony bucktooth grin, clasps my hand like a team member on the sidelines, itching for court time.

More insect buzzes in the air. The sudden BOOM! of a tank shell. The whole front of the building is covered in smoke, a big gaping wound pummeled into it. I can only imagine the state of the people in there. A sick smell of burnt rubber. Rifle innards grinding together, oil smoothing the friction, barrels spitting their bile. Kids cutting barbed wire for souvenirs. My God. I'm trembling. Jesus fucking Christ. Maria's disappeared again. It's her style. I steel myself and it comes out in these Beavis and Butthead giggles. I hate you, Anthony.

"José!" Simon. "There's something going on on Kalininsky. I've got what I need here. You wanna go?"

"Breakin' the law, breakin' the law." Simon loves British and American heavy metal. I can't think of a Clash song anyway under the circumstances, so I lay him a riff of Priest.

"Davai. Let's go. Rock and roll."

We dart in and out of the crowd, getting quotes. People react a little strangely to this leather-jacketed American with glasses, asking them questions about what they've seen. But they answer. People always want to talk. You just scratch the surface and it gushes out. Suddenly there's some flare-up to our left.

"José!" Simon. "Look!"

In the distance, on Novy Arbat, a scene from some Beirut news flash. An APC spins wildly under fire, bullets ricochet as the crowds scatter.

"Ace of Spa-a-ades! Ace of Spa-a-a-des!"

And off we go, at a run, darting in and out of a tree-lined area. Flashbacks of Ft. Chafee. Cover. Stay in cover. Stay camouflaged. The environment is your weapon, your best defense.

Snipers. They're posted at various windows in these highrises. They wait for the soldiers, the crowd to come out, and they knock off two or three targets before slipping back out of sight. It's my *Full Metal Jacket* nightmare. The troops always respond too late, with overwhelming force that demolishes the window where the sniper used to be a minute before. Meanwhile, he repositions for another shot. Simon is interviewing some prisoners of war, lying prostate on the ground.

A lull. My eyes are flitting everywhere, my trembling has gotten worse. Oh God oh God oh God. These people are xenophobes. I obviously look foreign, or at least "post-Soviet." The crowds are wandering free again, wide open, standing on the streets, looking up at the damaged buildings. The soldiers are antsy. One stands right by me, holding his weapon at the ready. Got the shakes. Simon hasn't seen what state I'm in. I'm sweating like a mother. Wedged in the space between two metal kiosks, I start fumbling about for the notepad in my bag. M-m-maybe I can ask these soldiers some questions? Get my mind off these shakes? Uh, h-h-how do you feel in this situation? What do you do in your spare time? H-how many rounds…

EXPLOSION.

My ears pop. Instantly, sound goes from silence to an off-the scale whine. I collapse onto the sidewalk, screaming, propped up against the brick wall. I'm shot. I'm shot. I'm… not. The soldier is firing his weapon. Less than two meters from me. Jesus, on the ranges we always wore ear plugs. There's a sniper on the building directly opposite, twenty soldiers are firing at his silhouette. Firing from all around me. Little flowers of dust blossom on the building's wall near the shadowy figure, inching closer, closer. Something inside me has jumped out, I grab myself, to make sure I'm not already dead. *Susto.* The firing continues ringing, ringing, in my ears, I stop them up with my palms, screaming.

Sustained crisis. That's the choice I pick on the Soviet Society final almost a year before."The former Soviet Union (I write), rather than sink back into authoritarianism, plummet into full anarchy, or successfully convert into a capitalist state, will instead find itself plunged again and again into a state of sustained crisis for several years, entailing..."

The sniper retreats back behind cover. It's obvious now that it wasn't a sniper at all, merely a dummy or something that remained in sight to draw fire. A decoy. An ammo waster. But it's hard to fire a Kalashnikov properly and think straight at the same time, especially when everyone else around you is rockin' and rollin'. You don't argue with bullets.

I'm throwing up. Spilling the last 24 hours all over the sidewalk, some on the soldier's boot. Heeeeeeeeeeeeeave. O-O-O-O-O-oh, fuck. I thought I was done with this crap.

The next thing I notice, I'm laughing, puke on my teeth, propping myself on all fours on the sidewalk. Man, if Drill Sergeant Chawyer Jones could see me now. Ha ha ha ha ha ha. The shakes are gone. Ha ha ha ha ha ha ha ha.

"Hey, Simon. Ha ha ha ha. *'The pins and needles prick the skin of little do-o-o-o-olls...'* Ha ha ha ha. Man, that scared the shit outta me. Simon? Yo."

Simon is shot. There is blood spurting from his side. The soldiers are all still looking up.

Fuck! Again I'm a non-thinking being. A being of action, of the training that takes me over, clear and unsullied after so much disuse. I am a medium through which the Army's first aid guidelines, hammered over and over over into me through so many boring sessions, perform their duty on my friend. My hands move on their own, willfully.

Apply pressure directly on the wound. Take a piece of cloth. Roll it into a ball. Place it over the wound and maintain pressure. With your free hand, take another piece of cloth and use it to secure the pad in place, wrapping it around the injured organ or body part. Add fresh layers to the pad and tighten the wrapping. Above all, prevent further blood loss. Prevent shock. Loosen the patient's clothing. Lift and secure his legs slightly above the level of the abdomen. If a sucking chest wound, do not give him anything to drink. Reassure the patient, if conscious. You may use phrases such as

"You're gonna be alright, buddy. Help is on its way. Hang on, Simon."

or

"You're gonna be fine. The doctors are coming. I've secured your injury and you're going to be fine, Simon. I'm right here with you."

Remember to address the patient by his name, as most people will find this reassuring. Repeat the phrases often. Keep him calm and confident that help is on its way and that the wound's bleeding has been stemmed. It is paramount that you yourself not give in to panic. Don't be a little pussy bitch, José. No te hagas joto. Follow your training and you'll always be all that you can be.

The Samaritans on stretchers come and take him away. Apparently it's not too serious. A rather deep flesh wound that might have grazed a lung, but they're confident that he'll have nothing more permanent than a nasty scar.

Long after he's gone, I find myself still breathing hard, my heart still pounding, the adrenaline rush just barely starting to ebb. The occasional sniper and retaliatory troop fire doesn't startle me. For some incredibly stupid reason, I no longer feel vulnerable. Dirty, dirty day.

I examine my bag, mercifully spared a barf bath, and find it's zipper hopelessly ripped. I have no idea how. Maybe it took a bullet. Another casualty. I turn a corner. Should get back to the paper. Armored cars still rushing past, more blasts of tank fire, crowds of curious coming out to see, living targets. I see a *bulochnaya* to my right, a bakery. Power's out, but they are open for business. Sales are brisk. I wait my turn in line and order a baguette. 1,500 roubles. *Spasibo.* Through the large window, outside, the war still rages, while inside here we all are, silhouettes buying bread, pastries, Folger's coffee packets. I chew the tip of my purchase and take in the view.

I bash Anthony's door open and kick out whoever he's talking with and really let him have it for ten minutes. You son of a bitch, you sent us on a suicide mission, how could you do that, you heartless, deformed bastard, this isn't some game to prop up your fucked-up ego, to make up for your shitty childhood and on and on and on. It's not worth recounting.

Anthony listens politely, staring now at the TV, now at the water cooler. In his own way, he really is a professional. He lets me get it all out 'til I'm spent.

I conclude with:

"Well. So, when's the deadline? Are we gonna have to get the stuff out early in case the printers get picky? Because of the *"prazdnik"* (holiday)? I guess you'll have to bribe them extra .."

"Yes. We'll need to have it ready to go by 11 o'clock. The city is under martial law as of an hour ago. Curfew is at 11:30."

"Right. Cheerio."

While I'm writing, Simon calls up from the hospital, sounding hale and hearty. He gives me his side of the story over the phone ("Hold on. I gotta wipe some blood from this asshole's last name"), and says he should be able to get out in a couple of days. "This was nothing compared to Nagorno Karabakh." Simon is a lieutenant in the Armenian air force reserve. "And José, one more thing."

"*Slushayu.* I'm listening."

"I know you're gonna write about this, everything that happened today, in your fucking columns and shit."

"… Yeah."

"Well, I don't want you to mention me. What happened to me. Plenty of other people have stories from today that you can write about. No offense, but I'm not fodder for your crappy stories that you can mold however you like. I'm me. You don't own me."

"Uh… sure, Simon. I-I-I didn't think that, uh, you know…"

"Yeah, yeah, never mind what you thought, you shit-for-brains. *Shto?* Ah. They said my wife just got here."

"Okay, Simon. I gotta write like the wind. Get well."

"Yeah, and José?"

"Yeah?"

"*FOR THOSE ABOUT TO ROCK…*"

We sing it together:

"*WEEEEE SA-LU-U-UTE YEWWWWWWW! BRRRRSCHSHS! BRR SHHHH!*"

4. ЧЕТЫРЕ

> "*No, mi Valentín querido, eso no sucederá,
> porque este sueño es corto pero es feliz*"
> — Manuel Puig, El Beso de la Mujer Araña

VOSVRASHAYUS
December, 1994. Back home in Texas. I hear this on the goddamned radio:

This is All Things Considered. *I'm Linda Wertheimer. Worldwide Media Watch released its annual report on foreign correspondents today. The group's statistics once again pointed to a troubling trend. More journalists and media workers working outside their home countries were killed in 1994 than in any other year on record. Since January, 128 of these journalists were killed in political and regional hot spots throughout the world, many in Eurasia. The latest media worker to lose her life on the job, 28-year-old photojournalist Cynthia Alston of Yonkers, New York, died two days ago while covering the ongoing conflict in Chechnya. Alston, a freelancer based in Moscow, was photographing damage in a civilian district of Grozny when the area fell under heavy shelling from a Russian mortar unit. This district of Grozny had no military significance, the unit's commander later conceded.*

Vosvrashayus. I'm going back. I cannot live here. Like Kurtz in *Apocalypse Now.* The jungle has changed me.

I'm going back. *Vosvrashayus.*

Datum was assassinated, more or less in the time frame Yuri had predicted. 11 slugs in his body, in a Moscow metro station 50 meters from the hotel. He wasn't wearing his vest. Others have also gone, my friend the poet Nina, of breast cancer. She was the heart and soul of a poetry circle I attended. She was, in many ways, my ideal of the "bohemian intellectual artist." Once we had a poetry reading on the eve of Epiphany in which we all impersonated figures from King Arthur's court. She was Morgan LaFey, dressed in a black dress with shards of mirror on it. It was all her idea. The cancer ate her almost all up. Her family couldn't afford proper medical care, and the Russian national health service is now shot to hell. She died in horrible pain, I was told. She was 38.

Vosvrashayus. I'm going back.

The ticket is bought, the goodbyes said. Roy has left me. I'm no longer "what he needs in his life." A trip out to LA to see him was a fucking disaster. My plane leaves tomorrow. There's nothing for me here. A boring nine to five job, I don't even want to say what. Freelance movie reviews for a local rag that edits them almost as bad as the *Post*. At least at the *Post* I could lobby Anthony directly for my versions, but here .. well, fuck it.

Fuck it all. *Vosvrashayus*. I'm going back.

Mi cuentito

Istoriia moia

My story. My story that is not over. My story that has not ended and never began. I'm boarding, I'm buckling up. I'm flying. I'm flying, in the air.

My story goes on, my story that has not ended and never began.

I'm going back.

Vosvrashayus.

BONUS MATERIALS

These news and other articles were written for the *Moscow Tribune* between 1993 and 1995.

THE MOSCOW TRIBUNE, TUESDAY, OCTOBER 5, 1993

Early Morning Show of Support for the President

By Jose Alaniz
The Moscow Tribune

In Monday's early morning hours, in the wake of the hardliners' seizure of the mayor's building and an horrendous attack on the Ostankino television centre, several thousand supporters of President Boris Yeltsin heeded a call by local leaders to come out and demonstrate, lending a morale boost to the president.

The motley group of elderly pensioners, juvenile rock fans and others descended on the Moscow City Council Building at Tverskaya 13, to meet the threat of communist revanchism.

"This is war," simply said one fatigue-clad young man atop an armoured personnel carrier on Pushkin Square.

By 3:30 a.m. Tverskaya had already been transformed into a surreal street-lamp-lit scene of some 5,000 supporters massed around the statue of Yuri Dolgoruky, the debris-strewn street sealed off on all sides by barricades made out of wood, pipes, cars, benches, and even giant Coke cans normally used for vending soft drinks. The air stank with the smoke of several fires surrounded by gaggles of people trying to keep warm.

The news coming through was still uncertain, some of it ominous. But two pensioners, Yuri and Galina Kaleado, remained steadfast.

"We are against fascists, against nazis, against Khasbulatov, against Rutskoi. These are the personification of the most foul thing in the world," said Galina, who with her husband had stood in the crowd for four hours by this time.

Despite the fact they were "old and weak," they conceded, the Kandelos felt that simply through their presence they were doing some good, even though some of their generation were actively and even violently for the other side.

"In these people's time there was much that was good, many blessings — many more than for normal people," Galina said of the hardliners. "And of course they don't want to lose those blessings, those comforts of life, so they try to hold on to those privileges which they'd made use of. And then also there's nostalgia for the past, for the order of the past."

Yuri admitted life is hard for them, but they weren't the only ones to consider.

"The fact is that it's not just about us having enough money today to buy food and not be needful in any way, but we also have children, grandchildren and we think about how they are going to live," he said. "And we think that if the communists rise to power, then our children's future will be a very dark future."

Sergei Martinov, some 50 years younger than the Kandelos, also thought of his one-and-a-half-year-old son as he took command of a platoon charged with guarding a barricade.

"We're not only defending the Kremlin, we're defending Russia," said Martinov, "so that my son, with God's help, will live normally, like a person — free. I simply hope that he'll live in a different time with different events than I did."

Vyacheslav Solovyev, an older platoon commander and daytime journalist, said he'd come out this morning because he wasn't sure the army could be trusted.

"We're ready to stand, as we did in 1991, and if someone comes toward us we'll try to answer them," he said. "The main thing is our presence here."

As the near-full moon rolled on to 4 a.m., Mossoviet leaders announced that two Army divisions had arrived in Moscow, with four more on the way. They had all sided with the president.

A cheer went up on Tverskaya in the early morning hours.

THE MOSCOW TRIBUNE, SATURDAY, OCTOBER 9, 1993

A Violent Conflict Shakes

They were images no one had wanted, and few expected, to see: Russian against Russian, violent clashes on the streets of Moscow, the White House in flames.

"We don't want blood," pleaded President Boris Yeltsin in an interview on Friday, Oct. 1. But by Sunday, the blood flowed freely from bodies battered by police truncheons and the fists of angry mobs.

Frustrated by a near-two week government blockade of the White House since Yeltsin's dissolution of parliament, a mass of hardline demonstrators took the fight to the police, who fell back overwhelmed. As a disconcerted world tuned in on CNN, 10,000 protesters flooded through the barricades and jubilantly joined their leaders holed up in the White House.

"We must take the Mayor's building and Ostankino!" railed fired vice president Alexander Rutskoi to his followers. Incited by his words, the crowds stormed their targets, taking the first and battling horrifically through the night for the second. Deaths already numbered in the dozens before the rumbling thunder of tanks once more echoed through the capital, for the first time since the 1991 Communist coup.

The White House goes up in flames on Monday after pro-Yeltsin troops began their attack.

Soldiers who had taken the side of the parliament sit in dejection after their surrender on Monday.

After two weeks of standoff, violence broke out Sunday with a bloody clash that ended in brief victory for White House defenders.

The Moscow Tribune

THE MOSCOW TRIBUNE, SATURDAY, OCTOBER 9, 1993

Page 5

Russia. But is it Over?

At about 9:50 a.m. on Monday, the furious response came to the violent mayhem caused by hardline mobs: tanks opened fire on the White House as troops assaulted the building. Masses of spectators, stretched as far back as Borodinsky Bridge, braved sniper fire to catch a glimpse of the action.

By the parliament's final surrender that afternoon, when hundreds of weary defenders slowly spilled out of the shattered building and Moscow still rattled with occasional sniper fire, the grim appraisal of damage had only begun.

As many as 200 had died in the worst Moscow violence since the 1917 Bolshevik Revolution; their funerals later in the week gave meaning to the term "Day of Mourning." Ironically, the violence may have claimed still another, larger victim: the last remnants of communism in Russia.

Awake, great Russia!
And anew, as before, get up from your knees
to a clear, open space!
Indeed this is not the first time you've had
to decide your fate!

— poet and hardline demonstrator Viktor Budarin, from a poem he wrote a week before the violence began.

Government troops patrol the grounds of the blackened parliament on Tuesday, while former vice president Alexander Rutskoi's dreams lie in shambles. (shown in the White House, insert).

The cost in the loss of human lives and shattering of families can never be reimbursed.

Adding to the surreal atmosphere of Sunday's events, spectators at the conflict sawed at pieces of barbed wire for souvenirs.

The Moscow Tribune

Curfew Paralyses Moscow Businesses

By Jose Alaniz
The Moscow Tribune

Oct. 7, 1993

In this year of living dangerously in Moscow, authorities see the 11 p.m. to 5 a.m. curfew in the city as a necessary measure to preserve order and safeguard lives in the aftermath of the weekend's minor war in the capital.

But to businesses and citizens used to operating late into the night, the curfew — in effect until October 10 — is more of an inconvenience than a blessing.

"It's basically shut us down," said Will Regan, co-manager of the new chic night club Manhattan Express, which opened only three days before the turmoil. "It's been a drag, but it just doesn't make sense to open and then have to have everyone out by 10 so they can get home. Opening for three hours just doesn't make sense economically."

The New York-style restaurant and night club does have business interruption insurance, although Regan suspected that, like most policies, theirs probably doesn't cover "acts of God" like war.

The club, located at the Rossiya Hotel, will open its doors and "try again" after the curfew is lifted, said Regan. In the meantime, the staff is using the down time to do inventory and receive imported supplies that were late anyway.

The all-night restaurant and club Night Flight on Tverskaya 17 is also taking advantage of the lull to do some renovation.

"We were going to do this work on the place anyway," said Manager Eva Sachs.

But Eduard Favinsky, owner of Bar Armadillo in the centre, complained that the curfew came at a bad time, just when his new Tex-Mex venture was getting popular.

"Half my business is gone," said Favinsky, who usually stays open until 5 a.m. and beyond. "I understand that we need this curfew for a few days, but I hope after that they'll stop it."

Bar Armadillo continues serving its guacamole and Mexican beer from 5 p.m. until just after 10 p.m., Favinsky said.

Jacko's Bar in the Leningradsky Hotel is serving free drinks during curfew hours.

Most casinos in the city — which thrive on late night crowds — have closed as well until the lifting of the state of emergency, some for economic reasons, others for safety.

"We've been closed since before the major stuff began to happen," said Tara Saracini, general manager of Casino Arbat at Novy Arbat 21, just up the street from the blackened shell of the White House. The area still echoes with occasional sniper fire.

"We mainly thought of the staff," said Saracini. "It's dangerous for them because of where we are. We're still coming in to keep an eye on things during the day, but we won't open until things quiet down."

This is the first time the president has declared a state of emergency in Moscow since August 20, 1991, when Communist hardliners unsuccessfully tried to seize power. Police force Lieutenant-general Alexander Kulikov, overseeing the state of emergency, announced on Russian television Monday that martial law would continue indefinitely, depending on how events developed.

Since then officials have announced the state of emergency would cease on Sunday.

The Moscow Tribune

THE MOSCOW TRIBUNE, TUESDAY, NOVEMBER 23, 1993

October Documentary Worth a Thousand Words

By Jose Alaniz
The Moscow Tribune

The images are already painfully familiar and for some, unforgettable: a blackened and burned parliament building, tanks rumbling through the streets of the capital, bulletfire lighting up the tense night when a country's fate hung on the actions of a tiny few.

Now, less than two months after the events of October's "second civil war," the Tsentr Television Company has produced a mesmerizing 30-minute documentary of those two days we all remember so well.

A Commemorative Report premiered Friday at the House of Writers to an audience of media workers, government officials and family members of those who died in the violence. It was a premiere unlike any other; audience members held lit candles during the screening and observed a moment of silence for the fallen. The hall was thick with emotion.

Made by journalists, and dealing chiefly with the experience of journalists who covered the fighting — and seven of whom died — the film achieves a poignancy and power all the more devastating for our proximity to the events.

"This is what we said, what we thought, what we lived in that time," said the makers of the documentary, essentially a pastiche of video footage from various local and foreign sources.

It's all there, in TV's magically encapsulating form: the riots and beatings that led up to the crisis, the tanks firing at the White House, the wounded frantically carried away under sniper fire.

Divided into four brief chapters, *A Commemorative Report* focuses most sharply on the death of TV journalist Yvan Skopan, who worked for the French company TF 1 and died from wounds received at the battle for Ostankino.

TF-1 bureau chief and Skopan's partner that night, Patrick Bourrat, describes the experience of helplessly hearing his friend's dying moans as the two were pinned down by relentless gunfire. In the documentary's most riveting image, Bourrat is shown crawling inch by inch along the street, pushing his camera ahead of him, to safety.

"I lost a friend. No reportage is worth the death of a reporter," said Bourrat, himself injured in the arm. "The only good is that through the death of Yvan and others we might understand a little better."

Another section deals with the camera subjects' reaction to being filmed. Many citizens attacked cameramen and reporters as "parasites", angrily covering up the lens with their fists and sheets of paper.

"Why does the camera call forth such rage?" the voiceover asks. "Why are we so afraid of seeing ourselves?"

Other coverage includes shots of people being treated at Sklifosovsky Hospital, the Ostankino fighting (with scenes shot by Skopan) and the evacuation of wounded in front of the White House. All the footage provides the closest, most chilling views of October's events yet seen.

But it's still mild compared to the reality, said director Dmitry Mochalin of Ostankino.

"There was a lot of footage that was just too horrible to put into the film," he said. "For instance, the footage from Sklifosovsky Hospital. The scenes we put in the film are not all that were shot. It wasn't that we were afraid to shock the viewer, but even to us it seemed too horrible."

Distilled from 20 hours of news reportage, *A Commemorative Report* assumes a knowledge — even an intimacy — with October's events and does not offer much by way of analysis. That is perhaps its only failing, though in its aggressive exploration of the emotions, the ultimate meaning, of the still-unbelievable images on screen, the documentary wins over its audience. A picture is, indeed, worth a thousand words.

"This was for the families, and actually, for everybody, so that they will understand what a journalist is," said Mochalin.

A Commemorative Report will be televised Nov. 29 on the Tsentr Television News Channel.

Caught between forces that would soon explode on Oct 3 These journalists are the subject of *A Commemorative Re*

MOSCOW CALLING

GARFIELD

TODAY'S CROSSWORD PUZZLE

MOSCOW STORIES

Dirty Day ...

By Jose Alaniz
The Moscow Tribune

If you want someone to blame/ Throw a rock and you'll hit someone guilty ... —U2

It's been almost six months, and by now just about everybody who has a story to tell from that day has told it. Close-call anecdotes and hardliner run-ins, stories of near-misses, of brushes with death, in the White House, in the Comecon building, at Ostankino. Some, like cameraman Yvan Skopan, didn't live to tell their stories.

Mine isn't as dramatic as many of those others — not having been trapped in the besieged parliament building, or caught in the television station firefight, or holed up in the mayor's captured offices. But it's been almost six months, and now's as good a time as any to tell it.

I distinctly remember that the day before I had put on my olive drab army underwear.

The little rustles of irony tingle through me now, but that morning there was really no way to know that I wouldn't be coming home that night — or, in fact, the next. It would be me and my standard U.S. armed forces issue against the year's scariest 48 hours.

I was in the office when the news broke. Sunday, Oct. 3. They were pouring over the White House barricades, where I'd been a number of times that week, covering the protests. The buzz-saw concertina wire, the gas trucks, the dog soldiers and metal shields. They were pouring through it. Ripping their clothes on the wire, playing bumper car battering ram with the trucks, pummelling the soldiers, taking the shields.

Live, on CNN. An angry ant army, smoke billowing. Live. The roused ants, stinging, screaming, washing over the bridge. on. Through the retreating troops. C. Through the flimsy barriers. N. Through to the White House, an angry ant hill, Live, bowled too many times. N.

"*Why are both you here?*" I asked Sergei and Volodya, our photographers on the scene at the wet, cold barricades. "*Fascists!*" screamed the crowd, a bubbling cauldron. "*There's two of us,*" replied Sergei with a sheepish grin, "*so if they kill one of us, the other will take his place.*"

There was no word from our photographers, or anybody else. But that was definitely the White House, those were definitely rioters, and it had definitely hit the fan. Live on CNN.

"Are we coming out tomorrow? Will we have an extra?" Such thoughts yielded to more important matters with the realisation that anybody caught in that streaming mob, particularly if they looked Western, was probably in it deep.

In come Jim and Lee, the Whitebread twins.

"We're lucky to be alive!" they kept on saying. "They were yelling 'Yankee go home!' They tore down the pictures at the Embassy compound! We turned around and there they were. We were swallowed up and carried away by this mob! There was gunfire all over!"

I called my friend Anatoly Borisovich, an intellectual sparring partner, to tell him any the news I was privy to. Live on CNN. His wife answered, said she'd get him. He never came to the phone.

We rushed out when we heard military vehicles thundering down Leninsky Prospekt in the eerie streetlamp-light. There they were. This was for real.

Courtesy of an amazingly calm cab-driver, I and some foolhardy Embassy staffers — who were absolutely forbidden from even sticking their necks out the window during this sort of event — went out to see the action at the Mossovict.

"This is war," said one young man in fatigues atop a tank.

Eventually I crashed at some friends' place near Mayakovskaya Square, still not really believing this was going on. I awoke about three hours later to the sound of my friend being interviewed over the phone long distance by her hometown's local news. Live. Not on CNN.

"It seems calm right now in a very beautiful dawn here in Moscow," she continued, and daybreak really was gorgeous, the best I'd ever seen — crystal colours almost audible with beauty. Was it made so by the crystal clarity of the moment, of a day that promised death, virtually guaranteed it? I sat in the 13th floor kitchen, saw the tanks below, and knew more blood would spill on this beautiful, beautiful day a'borning.

"*Why do you punish me so, Lord?*" wailed the old woman, hugging a tree in the wake of the protesters, driven back by police truncheons. "*I've suffered so, for so long. Why? Why?*" The cold drizzle continued, as two men stood far behind the woman, grinning in amusement. Live. Not on CNN.

A bottomless blue sky, air crisp and cold and delicious. The dirty day is here.

Maria, Simon and I head out to work, from the flickering television image. Live on CNN, to it's thrown-up version magnified a billion times: the White House, black smoke, the spectators come to watch the gladiatorial games.

Maria, a veteran of several Caucasus flare-ups. Simon, an Armenian who'd seen his share of the fighting. And me, an ex-Army reservist who'd never been under any fire that wasn't on a shooting range.

We push and "*Ameri*kanskii correspondent!" our way to within a hundred metres. Maria, in her photog's vest and sunglasses, gets even closer. She seas scrambles back, head bowed low, a sour look on her face.

"This is crazy," she says, "In a real war you more or less know where the bullets are coming from. But here, these people are firing whichever way they want. This is the most dangerous thing I've ever done."

Boy, does that do wonders for my confidence. Even *Maria's* worried, and the insect-like buzz of flying metal — sounding close enough to breathe on — inspires yet more dread. To top it off, we've taken cover behind a gas truck. Say, I think, *what if a bullet hits? What if there's gas in here? Um...*

People run by with stretchers, carrying wounded. Live on CNN. Simon's on the grass, talking to some shifty-eyed guy he says is a deserter from the parliament side. Others lie casually on the green, pointing out the sights to each other. A sick ozone smell of burnt rubber. Rifle innards grinding together, oil smoothing the friction, barrels spitting out their bile. Kids cutting barbed wire for souvenirs.

Maria has disappeared. It's her style. Simon and I rush back to the bridge, herded together with the sight-seers. We hear a flare-up over on Novy Arbat. I see an APC spinning wildly under fire. We run straight for it, in and out of trees. Flashbacks of Ft. Chafee coming at me.

Simon goes to talk to some prisoners held under guard, lying prone on the ground. I content myself with "professional observation," leaning against a kiosk. Suddenly, BOOM. The firing erupts all around me; I grab myself 'cuz for all I know I'm already dead. The soldiers by me are shooting up at a sniper. I can see him, his shadowy silhouette on the roof of a building. Little flowers of dust sprout up all over the wall near the figure, getting closer, closer.

Sustained crisis. That was the cliche I'd picked on the Soviet Society final, almost a year before. The former Soviet Union [I wrote]. *rather than sink back into authoritarianism, plummet into anarchy, or successfully corner into a capitalist state, will instead find itself caught in a state of sustained crisis for several years, entailing ...*

The sniper retreats, back behind cover. The shooting stops. I go into a *babushensa*, buy some bread for me and Simon. Business is brisk. More APCs are coming up the street. An old woman waves them back, helpless, like a mother scolding children that do not heed her. The metal shells rumble on. Live on CNN.

We wander back towards the parliament building, through a side street. I chomp on a banana I'd brought. My bag's zipper is broken, a casualty of this dirty day.

I see my friend Greg, a wire correspondent, dressed incongruously in a dark tweed jacket and long scarf, a Canadian Dr. Who.

"Where's there a phone?!" he asks, scowling, stalking by. "There's no phone around here!"

April 1, 1995

8 **The Moscow Tribune**

Former Reporter Vanishes in Crash

By Funky Wimberstein
Special to The Moscow Tribune

SOCHI — Authorities on Friday declared a former *Moscow Tribune* reporter missing after the plane he was riding in made an emergency landing in the Black Sea due to engine failure.

Jose Alaniz, who worked at the *Tribune* from May 1993 to June 1994, disappeared in rough waters as the plane meant to return him to Moscow after almost a year sank within view of the coastal resort of Sochi.

"We rescued everyone else on the passenger list from the sea," said local fisherman Vitaly Kissov, "but the American journalist just vanished."

It was just one more in a long list of obstacles — political, physical, bureaucratic — encountered by Alaniz in his six-month bid to return to Russia and resume his job on the *Tribune* staff.

These hurdles included, but by no means were limited to, visa troubles, unruly phone receptionists at the Russian consulate in New York, a paralysing addiction to American television, and a long bout with the debilitating "Generation X" disease, slackeritis, according to one of Alaniz's closest Moscow friends.

"He was really p-ed off about all the delays. He really wanted to come back," said sports editor Danny Wilkins, who spoke with Alaniz by phone shortly before his flight out of Houston. "I remember he said, 'All I need now is for the damn plane to crash.'"

Wilkins shared an office — coined "The Locker Room" by Alaniz in one of his columns — with the missing reporter, and maintained infrequent contact with him through the mail and telephone. These letters and conversations, Wilkins said, detail a sad extended nightmare of booze, inactivity, Gump mania, depression, Beavis and Butthead marathon weekends and other symptoms of "Russia withdrawal" in Alaniz's South Texas hometown.

The sometime journalist planned, upon his return to Moscow, to resume his unpopular, ranting column "Jumping Bean Blues" and equally annoying comic strip "Moscow Calling," as well the delusional weekly reviews "Videolog" and "Ah, the Humanity". Terrorism has not been ruled out in the airplane's emergency landing.

But those who knew Alaniz said it would take more than mere accidents or good taste to stop the intrepid, self-important Texan.

"I wouldn't count him out just yet," said Wilkins. "If I know Jose, he'll claw his way back here somehow. Anyway, I hope he does. He promised to bring me a copy of Henry Rollins' *Get in the Van*.

In a late development, reports have started to trickle in about a mysterious Western hitchhiker thumbing his way north from Sochi.

"He was mumbling incessantly," said Natalya Startnova, a local witness, "He went on and on, muttering, 'I'm coming, heh heh heh, going to Moscow, heh heh heh, this is gonna be cool.' He sounded like a complete imbecile."

Startnova's account placed the enigmatic figure some 800 miles south of the capital as of press time.

Student Identity Card
ISIC
ALANIZ
Date of Issue
18JAN68
6JAN93
USA
№
Хосе
Аланиз
“THE MOSCOW
TRIBUNE”
XX
ММКФ
Пресса
Press

José Alaniz, professor in the Department of Slavic Languages and Literatures and the Department of Cinema and Media Studies (adjunct) at the University of Washington, Seattle, has published academic books on Russian/Eastern European comics, disability in comics and superheroes. He also writes fiction and makes comics, including for the collections *The Phantom Zone and Other Stories* (Amatl Comix, 2020), *The Compleat Moscow Calling* (Amatl, 2023) and *Puro Pinche True Fictions* (2023, FlowerSong Press). He was born and raised in Edinburg, TX, right in the heart of the Rio Grande Valley. From 1993-1994 he lived in Moscow, Russia, working as a reporter and cartoonist for the *Moscow Tribune*, a local English-language newspaper launched by Anthony Louis. He continued to write intermittently for the Tribune until 1997.